F--k Boy

2

Nia Rich

Also by Nia Rich

Triangles

Never Going Back

My Love Is Deeper

Lovers Remorse

Seduced by a Savage

F—k Boy 2

Written by: Nia Rich
Copyright © 2017 Nia Rich

All rights reserved.

Cover: Tina Louise

Previously in F—k Boy….

"Hol'up baby don't move. I don't want to cum yet." Wes whispered in my ear. His head was rested on my shoulder while he laid on top of me. He was trying to catch his bearings. I rolled my eyes up to the ceiling. I swore his freak came out when he was drunk off some Hennessy. He would want to be in me all night, and I wasn't feeling it. I was hoping that it would be a quickie. I should have known better when I watched him take his third shot of Hennessy.

He kissed my shoulder, my neck, and then my lips. He stuck his tongue into my mouth. I could taste Hennessey on his tongue as he gave me a passionate tongue kiss that I didn't want. He began to pump in and out of me again at a slow motion until he felt like he had control.

Then, he started pounding more aggressively. He put my legs over his shoulders and plunged even deeper into me. Usually I would be screaming when he did that, but I wasn't there mentally. The sound of my headboard hitting the wall was more entertaining than him. I wasn't feeling it. At that moment, I knew that I had checked out of the relationship with Wes.

I honestly wanted to lay there like a dead fish until he got his, but since it was our four- year anniversary I decided to participate a little bit. He did take me out to dinner and a movie, so I mustered up some energy to moan a little for him. I also figured it would help him hurry up and cum, so he could get off me. I was trying to make him cum quick before he stopped me the first time. I wanted to get it over with, but he was steadily trying to make love to me.

Ugh would you hurry up and cum, so I can go to bed. I thought. Ava would be up in the morning, and I would be the one to get up with her. She was nine-months and she was sleeping through the night finally. Wes slept all morning before he had to go to work, so I would be up feeding, changing diapers, and chasing her around the house.

"Damn this pussy good baby." He moaned in my ear. I kept my eyes on the ceiling. He was finally about to come. Before he pulled out, he told me that he loved me. Once he laid down next to me, I got out of bed and went straight to the bathroom to take a shower.

"Bae where are you going?" Wes asked.

"To take a shower." I said.

"You couldn't lay with me for a second?"

"Yes, after I get cleaned up. I am sweaty Wes." I said with little emotion. I looked at my engagement ring again. I was trying to hold us together for our baby, but I couldn't take it anymore. I was still trying to dig myself out of a financial hole because of him. I was barely holding on to my house, my car, and my business at that point. The little that he was bringing in from his temporary job was helping a little, but the job assignment was about to end. I wasn't sure if I wanted him in my house when it did. I would be digging myself an even deeper hole if he was. Especially if he didn't get put on another job right away. Plus, he was coming home late and drunk again. Some nights he would be talking crazy to me. Other nights he would wake Ava up because he was loud, then, he would pass out and leave me to deal with her.

I felt a strong urge to go back into our bedroom and tell him that I was done. I didn't want all the ruckus he would cause if I did that, so I just closed my eyes and allowed the hot shower water to ease my stress. A few minutes later, I heard the bathroom door open. Wes came into the bathroom and got in with me. He was trying so hard to be romantic with me, but I couldn't get into it. *I should have locked the door.* I thought.

"You know I love you, right?" he said to me. It took everything in me not to roll my eyes at him.

"Really Wes?" I asked sarcastically.

"Really Adara? Your questioning my love?"

"I am questioning why you do the things that you do?"

He sighed, "What are you talking about bae? I ain't doing nothing but going to work and coming home to my girls."

"Are you sure?"

"Bae stop. Why are you trying to ruin this night with your questions? Yes, bae I am sure. I love you. I ain't got nothing else going on."

"Ok, but you're drinking a lot again."

"No, I am not. I was drinking with you tonight. Are you gonna put every little thing I do underneath a magnifying glass?"

"That is not what I am doing. Tonight, is not the only night that you have been drinking."

"Look, can I at least wash your body babe?"

"No, I am getting out."

"Aw that's cold Adara. Are we still going out tomorrow?"

"Yes."

"Aight cool. I bought you something that I would like for you to wear."

"What?" I asked while drying off.

"You'll see."

***

Although I wasn't feeling Wes, it did feel good to be out. I hadn't been out and feeling sexy in a long time. If I wasn't at home changing poopy diapers, I was at the shop standing on my feet for hours. He surprised me with tickets to a Tank concert, and an outfit to wear to the concert. The dress fit perfectly. I had finally gotten my body back to the way I like it, so I was feeling myself. I was having a great time with Wes. We danced, and we laughed, and he wasn't drinking. I guess because I had mentioned it the night before. I was happy that he decided to be on his best behavior. It felt like old times, and I could see why I fell in love with him.

"Excuse me! What the fuck are you doing here with this bitch Wesley!" I heard Lesley's squeaky voice yell from behind us. Wes and I were walking through the parking lot to our car. Both of us turned around.

"Hello!?" she yelled.

"Lesley go on with that bullshit." Wes said.

"Did you tell that bitch that you were with me the other night Wes!?"

"That bitch is standing right here! You can address me by my name if you have something to say to me!" I yelled.

"Shut the fuck up bitch!" she yelled.

"No, you shut the fuck up!" I yelled.

"Lesley chill out!" Wes yelled at her.

"Fuck no Wes! You told me that you were done with her!" she yelled at him.

"Well you can see that he's not." I said and flashed my engagement ring.

POW.

The bitch swung and hit me right in my head. "Bitch!" I yelled. I started swinging. She punched me a couple of times and I punch her a couple of times and then I got a hold of her hair. I kept punching her in her head. She kept swinging on me but she wasn't landing anymore punches. I was dragging her around that parking lot by her hair. People started crowding around, watching and recording the fight. All I was thinking about was killing that bitch. I didn't think about the fact that I could possibly be on YouTube, Hood Fights, or World Star. That bitch was gonna know not to ever fuck with me again. I had her hair in one hand and I kept punching her with the other. She was struggling to try to get up off the ground and pry my hands from her hair. I could hear Wes and some other people trying to break it up. I didn't know how long I was fighting. I had blacked out. That bitch was gonna pay for all the bullshit that she had been talking. I was handling her like I was one of the WWE Divas. Wes was finally able to pull me away from her. I kicked her in the chest when he pulled me away from her.

"Bitch I told you I would drag your ass!" I yelled. I had blood dripping from my lip. I spit it on the ground. Somebody was holding her. I wasn't sure if they were people that she knew, or people from the audience that we drew around us. Wes damn, near carried me to the car, forced me inside, and pulled off. All the while, I was still yelling across the parking lot about how Lesley had me fucked up. My adrenaline was pumping, and I could feel my heart was beating hard and extremely fast. I started yelling at Wes.

"You got me fucked up Wesley! You're still fucking that bitch!" I started to cry. "You got me fighting bitches over you! Look at my lip!" I looked down at my nails and two were broken. One of them was broken down to the skin. It was bleeding and my finger was throbbing.

"Look at my fucking nails!"

"Bae I'm sorry! She was lying! I don't know what was wrong with that bitch babe!"

"I have never had to fight a female over a guy and you got bitches attacking me!" I pulled down the visor mirror to look at my lip.

"Look at this shit! Wes!"

"Bae calm down! That chick was out of pocket!"

"Fuck calming down! You're still cheating on me Wesley! I'm done! I don't want to do this anymore!"

"Bae!"

"I don't want to hear shit!"

We pulled up to my mom's house, so we could pick up Ava.

"I'm done! I'm staying here!" I said when he parked in front of my mom's house. I jumped out of his car. He jumped out of his car too and darted over to me. He grabbed me to hold me to stop me from walking, but I pushed him off me and started swinging at him. "Get away from me Wesley!"

He was blocking my punches with his arms and trying to grab me at the same time. I whopped him upside his head a couple of times. "Adara Stop!" he yelled. He grabbed both of my arms and pulled me to him to restrain me. My back was up again his chest and he had my arms folded in front of me.

"Baby stop. Ok. Stop. Please. I love you. calm down." he said into my ear. Both of us were out of breath.

"I've been calm. I've been calm for too long Wes. It's all my fault because I keep letting you do this to me. I'm done. I'm staying here."

"Adara listen baby, you are tripping right now. Let's go home and talk about this."

"I am done talking about this! I'm done! You have to go!" I yelled and started struggling to get away from him.

"Stop Adara! I ain't going nowhere!"

"Yes, you are!"

My mom heard us and came to the door. "What's going on out here? It's late."

I stopped moving.

"We are alright mom; I am about to come in." I said. "Let me go Wes." He released me and stepped back.

"I don't know what is going on, but you are making too much noise out here."

"Here I come mom."

I turned to him and said, "Be gone when I get home. Get all of your shit and get out." He had tears in his eyes. He looked like he wanted to say more, or put up a fight, but he didn't.

"I'm sorry Ms. Lewis." He said and walked back to his car, got in, and pulled off.

"What happened to you? I know that he didn't put his hands on you." My mom said with a look of concern on her face.

"No mom. I got into a fight with a chick at the concert." I said as I walked into her house.

"Oh, my goodness, girl you know you are too cute to be fighting."

I shook my head. I did know that I was too cute to be fighting over some raggedy ass dude. I was still stunned by the whole ordeal. I told my mom all about what happened. Once I was done explaining the whole thing, I said, "I'm done mom. I can't do it anymore."

I meant it that time. I spent the night at my mom's. She drove me home the next day. Wes was gone. He took all his stuff as I asked, and he left peacefully. I'm glad he did because I just didn't have it in me to deal with anything else. My mom and I walked through the house to make sure everything was alright before we put Ava down onto her feet. As I walked through my house, I realized how relieved I was to see my closets clean and free of Wes's things. At that moment, I knew that I was done. I was tired, I was down to my last, and my patience was gone. I had given everything I had until I had nothing left to give. Wes was a fuck boy, and I was the woman who loved him. I put up with Wes because I love him, but I couldn't deal with it anymore. That fight with Lesley put the nail in the coffin for him. I loved Wes with all my heart and soul. All I wanted, was for Wesley to do right, so we could be together forever. In the process, I allowed Wes to almost ruin my life. I put all my focus into Wesley, and lost sight of Adara. It was time to get my life back and let my fuck boy go.

A month later:

Wesley: Adara, I know that you hate me. I would hate me too. I should have done better. I could have treated you better, but I didn't. I made a lot of mistakes I know that can't be erased. I admit, I was lazy about getting and keeping a job. I let my drinking get the best of me, and I apologize bae. I need you baby. I ain't right without you. I miss you and my daughter. I pray every day that you will forgive me and give me another chance.

Adara: I'm Good.

I was, and I had never felt better.

F--k Boy

2

Nia Rich

Nia Rich

ADARA

Chapter 1

I put Ava in her bed, and then I walked into my kitchen. I poured a glass of red wine, walked into my living room, and sat down on my couch. It was another night with just me and my baby. A night with just me and her was a lot better than another night with Wes worrying me to death. I got comfortable on the couch, and then my phone started ringing. Without looking at it, I knew that it was Wes. He hadn't stopped calling since we'd broken up. I didn't feel like being bothered by him that night, so I let the phone ring through to voicemail.

After the fight with Wes's side chick Lesley, I was done with him. I couldn't do it anymore. It took a few days for the swelling from my busted lip to go down. It took a month for my broken nail to heal. It hurt so bad. Especially anytime that it got wet. I had to wear a band aid on it for two weeks. That bitch Lesley called my salon several times harassing me and putting threats on my life, but she never showed up. My whole staff was ready for her, if she did decide to make an appearance at my salon again. I ended up getting an order of protection on her. I had Wes's number blocked for about two months. He was talking to me through my mom and his mom until our moms convinced me that Wes and I needed to at least be cordial for our daughter. They were the only reason I unblocked his number. I was prepared to raise our daughter by myself without him in our lives.

I took a gulp of the red wine I was drinking and thought about how Wes messed everything up with us. I wished that he would have done right. I felt like I hated him for what he did, but I still loved him. I was still thinking about him all the time. I hadn't even moved on yet. I wasn't interested in dealing with another man. I didn't want to be bringing different men in and out of my daughter's life. It was supposed to be Wes, Ava, and me. I felt like he destroyed the family portrait, so I had to be fine with doing it all alone.

I took another gulp of wine and heard my phone ringing again. I knew that it is Wes again. He always called a second time when I didn't answer. Every time he called, he asked about Ava, and then he turned the conversation from our daughter to the possibility of us getting back together. I rolled my eyes, and then I answered the call.

"Hello?" I asked.

"Sup Adara? Where is my princess?"

"She's asleep. You know that."

"I didn't know that."

"It's nine o'clock at night Wes."

"Well, how is she?"

"She is fine."

"Aight. What you doing?"

"Wes what do you want?"

"You know I miss you baby."

"Um hum."

"When are you going to stop being so mean to me? It's been a year and I'm still trying to make things right with you."

"Stop trying."

"Damn, Adara it's like that?"

"Yes. Now you can go back to that bitch you're fucking."

"Why do you always got to bring up other women. I already told you there ain't no other bitches. There is only you. You are the only woman that I want to be with."

"Um hum."

"Aight. I'm going to talk to you later. I love you baby."

I didn't respond or say good bye. I just hung up. I took a deep breath and exhaled. I was in my feelings as usual after I talked to Wes on the phone. I'd been letting his mess weigh me down for too long. It was time for me to get back to my life. I just didn't know how to move on, but I knew that I needed to do it.

Chapter 2

"Are you ready to fly out to N.Y. for this wedding this weekend girl?" Nikita asked me before taking a sip out of her bottle of orange soda. We were at the salon, and I was cutting and styling her hair for Chanel's wedding.

I turned the clippers I was using off and set them on my station. I picked up a brush and said, "Not really, but I don't have a choice. Chanel would kill me if I don't show up."

"Cuz you have to get out that funk and be happy for Chanel. She is not my most favorite person in the world, but I'm still happy for her uppity ass. Plus, I will not turn down a free trip to New York. Ok girl."

I laughed. "I feel you, and I am not in a funk either."

"So, why haven't you started dating yet girl? It's been a year since you and Wes broke up.

"So."

"So, it's time to get some new dick. You know that is the best way to get over old dick." Nikita said.

"Girl shut up. You need to get some new dick. Didn't you just catch Jakari cheating again?"

"Yea, but he promised that he was done this time."

"He says that every time. How many times are you gonna give him another chance?"

"This is the last time cousin."

"Um hum. You said that the last time. Girl you're gonna mess around and let him give you something incurable."

"Whatever."

I looked at her through my station mirror and said, "I'm just saying. It's time to let that go."

"Anyways. We're not talking about me. I got me figured out. We are talking about you."

I rolled my eyes at her. "Um hum." I said. She was getting on my nerves because she knew that I was speaking the truth, but she refused to listen.

"You're still in love with Wes, aren't you?"

"No."

"I don't believe that cousin."

"He is not going to do right, so there is no need to care."

"Yea. You're still in your feelings."

I put the brush down and picked up a comb and a small curling iron. "Anyways. How do you feel about our bridesmaid's dresses?" I asked. I needed to change the subject. I didn't want to stand there and talk about Wes while I was doing everything in my power to forget about him.

"They are cute, and mine fits my big tits real nice. You know how those type of dresses can be sometimes. They never make them for women with big breasts."

"Yea but, I ain't feeling the color she picked. Who picks black to be there wedding color anyways?"

Nikita laughed. "Shit your boujee ass friend."

"People wear black to funeral's not weddings."

Nikita laughed some more. "Wow I've never heard you throw shade towards your *sister*. Most of the time you're putting her on a pedal stool."

"I'm not hating. I'm just stating the obvious."

"Sounds like a little hate to me." Nikita said and then she drank some more of her orange soda.

I laughed and said, "Shut up."

Nikita put the bottle on my station and said. "I kind of like it. Shade looks good on you."

"I'm done with you right now cousin."

"Maybe we'll meet some cute guys out there this weekend. I'm ready to get lit."

"Oh, you're trying to wild out?" I asked.

"Hell yea. Fuck Jakari this weekend. Out of sight out of mind."

"And what is that going to solve cousin?"

"Nothing. It's just going to make me feel good. What Jakari doesn't know won't hurt him."

"You're crazy cousin." I said.

I took my phone out of my apron to text message my mom. I wanted to make sure she didn't forget that she was taking Ava for the weekend. I was happy that my mom agreed to take her, so that I didn't have to worry about tussling with her and her diaper bag all weekend.

I sent the text message, put the phone back into my apron, and started sweeping up Nikita's hair from around my station. Nikita was staring at herself in the mirror checking out her hairstyle that I'd just finished.

"This is nice cousin. Thank you."

"You're welcome."

"Hey ladies!" Kyra said when she walked into the salon.

She was one of my new stylists. Kyra is tall with small breast and wide hips. She wears her hair natural and she doesn't wear a lot of make-up. Bianca introduced her to me. She and Bianca were close and had been knowing each other for a while. I was glad Bianca brought her along. She was a great asset to my salon. She brought business to the salon, and I loved her energy.

"Where is Bianca?" Nikita asked while still looking in the mirror.

"I don't know. She told me that she was on the way here. We both have clients in about thirty minutes." Kyra said.

"Oh ok."

"Are you two, ready for that wedding this weekend?"

I pointed at Nikita and said, "She is."

"Why aren't you?" Kyra asked.

"I'm ready to meet this mystery guy that my sister is about to walk down the aisle with." I said.

"Oh. You haven't met him yet?" Kyra asked.

"No. She has been keeping him a secret. I hope that it's someone good."

"I feel you. It's natural to be concerned about your loved ones when they are taking a big step like that."

"Are you, Bianca, and Deon going to be ok with holding down the fort for a few days?" I asked Kyra.

"Absolutely boss lady. We got this." Kyra said.

"Thank you."

Bianca walked in and said, "Hey y'all!"

I said, "Hey girl."

"Before I forget, tell your girl congrats on the marriage." Bianca said.

"I will. I'll be right back. I need to take this call." I said.

I walked to my office in the back of the salon and answered my phone.

"Are you going to let me see you before you leave for N.Y.?" Wes asked after I answered the phone.

"No."

"Why not?"

"Because I don't want to see you, but you can go and see your daughter. She will be with my mom."

"I'm tired of seeing our daughter at your moms. It's always your mom playing the middle man. I want to see you and my daughter."

"Well. It's not going to happen."

"I miss you."

"I don't care."

"I love you."

"I don't want to hear that."

"You're still my future wife."

"No, I'm not."

"That's what you say out of your mouth, but you know the truth."

I sighed loudly. "The truth is. I'm done with you Wes. I'm not sure when it's going to sink in for you."

"I'm tired of going through your mom to see my baby. I want to stop by and see my baby when you get back. Can you at least let me do that?"

"You're not stopping by my house."

"Ok, well, we can meet somewhere."

"I'll think about it. I have to go." I said and then I hung up. I walked back into the salon, cleaned up my station, and then Nikita and I left.

Chapter 3

I rang the doorbell to the New York mansion, and then Nikita and I waited for Chanel to answer it. We surveyed the circle driveway, the expensive cars parked in the driveway, and the immaculate lawn.

"This place is huge." Nikita said.

"It is." I replied.

"Sister!" Chanel exclaimed when she opened the door.

She opened her arms to hug me. "You look gorgeous sister." she said.

"So, do you." I said to her. She let go of me, and hugged Nikita, and then we followed Chanel into the house.

I'm sure Nikita was shocked at how friendly Chanel was being to her because I sure was. I was happy that my sister was feeling good and there was no negativity between the two of them.

"This house is amazing sister." I said as we walked through the house.

"See I told you." Chanel said.

"I see." I said.

"Everything will be set up in the back for the wedding, and then the reception will be in this room." Chanel said as we followed her through the house to the huge dining room area. It was half way set up for the reception, but there was still a bunch of decorating to be done.

Nikita said, "Wow. I have never been in a house this big.

"I knew you ladies would love it. I will give you a full tour when the rest of the ladies get here." Chanel said. "Let's sit and talk for a second."

We followed her to the kitchen and sat down at the kitchen island.

"Wine or Champagne?" she asked.

"Let's do wine. I'm sure that we will be drinking plenty of champagne in the next few days." I said.

"Wine it is." Chanel said.

She pulled out a couple of bottles of white wine out of a bottle holder, and she took several glasses out of the cabinet. She set everything on the table and said, "Just wait until the bachelorette party. I have a good friend planning it. Trust me, you guys are not going to forget it."

"Yes. We're going to get you wasted." Nikita said.

Chanel laughed as she popped the cork out of an expensive bottle of wine.

"The other ladies should be here soon." Chanel said.

I asked, "Where is the man of the house?"

"He will be here soon as well." Chanel said.

"Good. I can't wait to finally meet this mystery man." I said. Chanel handed both of us a glass of wine and then poured one for herself.

"Are you nervous?" Nikita asked.

"A little. Normal wedding jitters. I just hope that I don't fall trying to walk down the aisle."

Nikita and I laughed and then we heard the doorbell ring. Chanel excused herself and walked to the door. I could see the rest of her bridesmaids standing on the other side of the large glass door.

"Hey!" I heard Chanel say when she opened the door. Each one of them spoke and hugged her.

"Look at you darling, looking all thin." One of her friends said to her. I recognized her. It was Chanel's best friend Melanie. I had never met her, but Chanel had told me about her. I knew that she dated ball players too.

Chanel replied, "Thank you." They followed her into the kitchen. She introduced everyone. After we shook hands, Chanel poured the rest of the ladies some wine.

"Adara it's great to finally meet you. I've heard so much about you." Melanie said.

"Likewise." I said.

I wasn't feeling her too much. She seemed a little too Hollywood for my style. Melanie was more boujee than Nikita says that Chanel is. She was extremely pretty and looked overly nipped and tucked. She had the flat stomach, the oversized booty, the platinum blonde extensions, the lips full of collagen, and the extremely long acrylic nails. I was over her as soon as I saw her.

"Chanel told me that you do hair. You should do mine one day." she said as she flicked her platinum blonde weave over her shoulder.

"Yes, I do. I own a salon. We will have to set that up."

"Ok!" Melanie smiled. I smiled back, but I was being fake.

I was not feeling her at all. I was never going to do her hair, even if my life depended on it. I can deal with Chanel's boujee ways, but that chick was getting on my nerves in just the little time that we spent together. Chanel looked at me like she could tell that I was being fake, but she wasn't going to address it, and then the sound of the garage door lifting caught her attention.

Chanel said, "My man is home. I'll be right back." She ran to the garage door and jumped into his arms as soon as he stepped into the house.

He said, "Hi baby."

Chanel said, "Hi babe. The ladies are here. Are you ready to meet them?"

He said, "Yea babe." I could hear his deep voice from around the corner. They walked back around the corner holding hands. I saw Melanie's eyes pop open when they stepped into the kitchen. His muscles were visible through the t-shirt he was wearing with a pair of khaki shorts. My face had no expression at all when I saw him. I was livid.

Chanel said, "Ladies, this is my soon to be husband Orlando King."

Her soon to be husband was one of the best and most popular wide receivers in the league, but he was also one of the biggest hoes in the league, and my ex-boyfriends' best friend.

Orlando said, "Hello."

All the ladies spoke except me. I just took a sip of my drink. My facial expression had not changed, and the look in my eyes told Chanel that I was not pleased at all. A smile spread across Melanie's face.

Chanel said, "I think you already know Adara, so this is Melanie, Nikita, Corine, and Jennifer."

"Well it's nice to meet you ladies, and welcome to our home. Make yourself at home. You can have anything you want in here. I got to get out of here, but I will see you ladies at the rehearsal."

He turned and kissed Chanel, and then he left. After the garage door closed, the ladies squealed.

"Oh my God. You are marrying fine ass Orlando King?" Nikita asked.

Melanie asked, "Why didn't you tell me!? He is finer in person than he is on television."

"Yes, he is!" Corrine said as she slapped hands with Melanie.

Chanel laughed and said, "Thank you." She looked at me, but I still wasn't saying anything.

"Will his friends be here?" Jennifer asked.

"Yes, they will. I am sure a lot of ball players will be here."

"Oh, shit girl. It's about to go down." Nikita said.

"Ok girl!" Jennifer said. She slapped hands with Nikita.

Chanel laughed and changed the subject. "You ladies are crazy. Let me give you a tour of our house." Everyone stood up with their wine glasses in hand and followed her.

***

Chanel had been waiting for the moment to pull me to the side to talk to me. I still hadn't said much since meeting Orlando, and I knew that she wanted to know why. She waited until we were at the meet and greet; while everyone was busy eating appetizers and talking. She quietly walked up to me, grabbed my hand, and pulled me with her down the hall into one of the bedrooms.

"Alright Adara. What's up? You haven't said a word all day." Chanel said.

I leaned back on one leg and folded my arms across my chest. "Orlando King sis? Donte's best friend?"

"Yes. What?"

"You know Donte used to run around with him when he was cheating on me with all them hookers. Orlando was fucking all those nasty bitches too and he was married at the time."

"So, people change sis." she said.

"Out of all the dudes in the league, you had to get with Orlando King? He will fuck your mama if she lets him, and you know he tried to get with me when I was with Donte." I said.

"He was a lot younger then. We love each other." she said.

"What does love have to do with you marrying a no-good ass dude?"

"Oh, you're one to talk. At least he has a career and money. You can't say the same about your baby daddy. Orlando takes care of me and gives me anything I want."

"I forgot that you will sell your soul for money. Is this why you kept him a secret? Because you knew that I wasn't going to be ok with this?"

"No, I kept him a secret so that no one would try to sabotage what we had going on. You know that he is popular. Seriously sis, I'm not trying to hear this right now. I'm not about to let your negative vibe ruin my wedding." Chanel said.

"Ruin your wedding? The fact that you know he has a reputation for being a hoe, has hella baby mama's, and kids should be enough to wreck your wedding. Are you going to be a step mom to all his damn children, or are you going to join the party and add to the clique of Bebe's kids?" I asked.

Chanel shook her head and said, "Whatever."

"Is Donte going to be here too?" I asked.

"Yes." she replied.

"And you couldn't warn me?" I asked.

"Sis I couldn't because then you would have figured out who I was marrying. I knew you were going to feel some kind of way, so I already prepared myself to deal with it."

I shook my head, and then I said, "You know you didn't give me a choice, and now I am stuck, and now I have to support you, even if I don't agree with you doing this."

"You don't sis. You can go back to the hotel, if you want to, and I will understand."

"You know that I am not going to do that."

"I know because regardless if you knew who I was marrying or not, you were going to support me because you love me."

"I do."

"Alright, so can you at least put your feelings about Orlando away and have a good time for me please?"

I inhaled and exhaled loudly. "Because I love you. I will, and I will also keep a shoulder available for you to come cry on when this dude starts fucking up."

"Thanks sister." Chanel smiled and opened her arms for a hug.

"Um hum." I said as I hugged her.

"Now come on let's go back and join the party."

Chapter 4

I was sitting at the wedding reception watching people get misty eyed while watching my sister dance with the biggest mistake of her life. I regretted showing up for the wedding. Chanel could have sent the bullshit to me via live stream. Better yet, she could have sent me a video clip through email. Not even through text to my phone, but to an email that I would never check. I would've rather been at home with my daughter, but I was stuck in New York with my ex, his hoe ass best friend, and my dumb ass sister. I wanted to feel happy for her, but I couldn't because I knew that dude too well. He was the biggest fuck boy of them all. The only difference was; he had money; lots of it. He was worse than my ex's Donte and Wes put together.

I felt Donte staring at me from across the room, but I did not give him eye contact or acknowledge his presence. I was praying that he didn't feel bold enough to approach me because I did not want to embarrass the both of us in front of all those people at the wedding. I looked at Chanel smiling and glowing as she danced with Orlando. She did look beautiful in her wedding dress. I started to feel like maybe I was being bitter because of my situation. Maybe Orlando's punk ass had changed. It *had* been some years since I was in a relationship with Donte. I gulped down the rest of the champagne in my glass, and then I took another glass of champagne from one of the waitress's walking around with trays of filled glasses.

I need to drink myself into this moment. I'll just drink, smile, and pretend like I am happy to be here. I thought.

"Girl this wedding is so beautiful." Nikita said.

"It is." I said.

Nikita said, "I wish Jakari would do something like this for me."

She had a dreamy look on her face. Nikita had gotten bit by the wedding bug like most women do when they attend weddings. There was no way that she could have been seriously thinking about a marrying Jakari. I ignored her Jakari statement and gulped down some more champagne. Everyone ate, and then the DJ got the party turned up. I watched as Chanel and Orlando made their way around the room. I stood near a wall while sipping champagne and text messaging my mom to check on my daughter. She told me that Ava was doing fine, and then I chatted with her a little about the wedding. By the time I looked back up from my phone, the dance floor was lit. The DJ played a popular Drake song that got everyone going. Nikita was out there dancing with one of Orlando's baller friends. She had her butt all up on his manhood twerking. I guess she wasn't lying about wilding out while we are there. Chanel was dancing with one of her cousins, and then I noticed Orlando talking to Chanel's friend Melanie. Melanie was standing too close and smiling way too much in my opinion.

I took another glass of champagne from the waitress. The alcohol had me thinking way too heavily about Wes. I drank down another gulp and then I heard a male's voice say my name. I looked up to see Orlando standing right in front of me.

He said, "What's up Adara? I haven't had the chance to talk to you. I wanted to thank you for coming through to support me and your girl."

"You're welcome. Congrats to you both." I said.

"Thanks. How have you been?"

"I've been fine."

"I heard you had a daughter. Congrats. Is the father in the league?'"

"Thanks, and no."

"You're still fine as ever."

"Thanks."

"You know that I still want you, so whenever you're ready." He gave me a lustful look.

My face frowned. *No, this mutha fucka didn't just hit on me at his wedding!* I thought.

"Excuse me?" I asked.

"I was clear, and you can tell her I said it. She will never believe you. Just let me know and I will handle that for sure."

"You better get the fuck up out my face Orlando, don't you ever come at me like that again." I responded angrily.

He chuckled and said, "Yea aight. I'll holla." Orlando turned and walked away.

I was pissed and disgusted and I was sure that the expression on my face said so. I knew that his hoe ass hadn't changed.

"What's wrong with you?" Chanel asked as she was dancing up to me. She had a huge smile on her face.

"Did Orlando thank you for coming?" she asked.

I wanted to tell her what had just happened, but she looked so happy that I didn't want to ruin her moment.

"Yea girl." I said.

"Good. I sent him over here to do so. Now come dance with me." She pulled me by the hand. I let her pull me to the dance floor with her. We two-stepped to, "Step in The Name of Love". I peeped Donte watching me again. I prayed that it would all be over soon, so he could be out of my presence.

"Ok I have someone who I want you to talk to." Chanel said.

"Who? I hope that it's not Donte."

"No girl."

"I hope that it's not any of Orlando's friends either."

"It's not. Chill out. He is a good friend of mine. I 've known him for years and he is a nice guy. He is a Doctor girl. He lives in Atlanta." Chanel said.

"Someone that you've dated?"

"Girl no. He is too boring for me. I would never date him. He is not my type. I admit he has dated one of my other friends, but it didn't work out. I think you two would be perfect for each other. He is also recently out of a relationship, and he also has a daughter the same age as your daughter."

"No girl. I don't know. I didn't come here for that."

"Gil please just talk to him. Please for me. It doesn't even have to go any further than this.

I sighed, and then I said, "Alright sis."

"Yes! Ok I'll be right back."

Chanel walked off the dance floor and across the room. I saw her talk to this tall and handsome guy with a deep brown complexion and dreads.

"Ok, well, she got the skin tone right." I said to myself. I watched the two of them walk back over to the dance floor. Chanel looked extremely excited to be introducing us.

Chanel said, "Ok. Adara I would like for you to meet Dr. Miles Nash."

I said, "Hello."

He extended his hand and said, "Hi nice to meet you."

"I'm gonna leave you two to talk." Chanel said and then she walked away.

He looked at me, and then he nervously chuckled a little before saying, "Um. I know this is awkward, but I told Chanel that I wanted to meet you. I have not been able to keep my eyes off you since I walked in the door. You are extremely beautiful."

"Thank you." I replied.

"She told me that you were single. I hope that is true. If not, let me apologize."

"She told you the truth. I am single."

"Alright great. Would you like to dance?"

"Well, we are already on the dance floor so."

"Right." he said, and then he chuckled nervously again.

We began doing a light two step. Nothing like what Nikita was doing with Orlando's friend. When the song was over, we got something to drink, and then we found somewhere to sit. I talked with him for the rest of the night. When the reception was over, we told each other that we were happy that we met, we would keep in touch, to have a good night, and then we went our separate ways.

Chapter 5

"How was the wedding?" Bianca asked.

"Yea, how was it?" Kyra asked as she walked to her stylist chair. She had just finished working on a client.

Nikita was in my chair. She wasn't getting her hair done. She was just hanging out. I was sure that she was there to gossip about the wedding and anything else the ladies wanted to talk about. She didn't have to be back to work until the next day and her son was with her mom.

"Girl it was lit!" Nikita said excitedly.

I said, "It was nice."

"Sounds like Nikita had a better time than you." Bianca said.

I laughed. "Trust me she did. She didn't make it back to our hotel room until the next morning."

"What!?" Bianca asked.

Nikita laughed, "Girl let's just say I was faded, he was fine, and rich."

"Aw shit." Bianca said.

"Yea, what happened in New York will stay in New York."

"Girl that statement is only good for Vegas." Bianca said.

"Well I made it for New York too." Nikita laughed. The rest of us laughed too.

"Don't try to sit here and act innocent Adara." Nikita said to me.

"What?" I asked.

"You know what. I saw you talking to dude the whole night."

Bianca's eyebrows went up, and the she asked, "Hold up, what dude!?"

"This little cutie with some dreads."

I laughed, "Shut up Nikita." I looked at my phone and ignored a call from Wes.

"Uh-uh. Talk." Bianca said.

"It wasn't that serious. Chanel introduced us. He is a doctor."

"A doctor?" Bianca asked.

"Yes. An attractive one. He was a gentleman. We talked, and then I went back to the hotel and went to bed."

"Tell us more about him." Bianca said.

"He is single, has one kid. A daughter the same age as mine. It didn't work out with the mother. According to him, she partied too much and wasn't committed to the relationship with him or being a mother to her daughter, so he currently has his daughter full time."

"Wow. That chick must have been stupid to fuck up with a doctor." Bianca said.

"Right." Kyra said.

"I know. That is what I was thinking."

"So, did you get his number?"

"Yea we exchanged numbers, but I don't think I am going to talk to him."

"Girl why?"

"I'm just not ready for all that yet."

"I told her that she is still not over Wes." Nikita said.

"Sounds like it." Bianca said.

"Whatever I am over him. Nobody is thinking about Wes."

"Um hum." Nikita said with a smile.

"So, you finally met her husband. What did you think?" Kyra asked.

"Girl I was pissed."

"Why?"

"Because he is my ex-boyfriends' best friend. He wasn't shit then, and he ain't now. I don't know why she would get with him out of all people."

"You didn't tell her that you were mad, did you?"

"Yes."

"No. On her wedding weekend?" Bianca asked.

"She asked, and I couldn't hold it in."

"It was written all over your face cousin." Nikita said.

"I thought I was being cool." I said.

Nikita laughed and said, "Um. No."

"Damn sis. You're ruthless." Bianca laughed.

"What did she say when you told her?" Kyra asked.

"She told me that she didn't want to hear it, and that she wanted me to be cool for her wedding."

"Which is only right." Bianca said.

"Did you?" Kyra asked.

"Yea." I said.

"Kind of." Nikita said.

"Shut up." I said and laughed. The door opened, and Kyra's client walked in. All of us spoke to the client, and then I excused myself to leave the front and go to my office to call Wes back.

When he answered the phone, I said, "What?"

He replied, "What?"

"Yea what do you want Wes?"

"Don't what me woman."

I sighed loudly, and then I said, "Wes, I am busy."

"I just wanted to see how New York was."

"It was fine."

"I bet you were looking good huh?"

"Wes."

"What? Send me a picture."

"I am about to go."

"Wait." he said.

"What?" I asked irritably.

"When are we going to get together, so I can see Ava?"

"Didn't you see her when I was gone?"

"Yea, but I told you. I want to see you and her. You said you would think about it."

"I did, and I think we are fine doing things the way we've been doing them."

"I am tired of going through your mom Adara. It has been a year now. We need to get past this."

"You don't get to tell me when we should get past anything Wesley."

He paused, and then he said, "Calling me by my full name Adara? Aight. You're tripping. I just want to make things right for our baby."

"Things are fine."

"Things are not fine, if her parents can't even see each other."

"We are cordial. We have worked out a system. We are fine. There are plenty of kids out here with parents who do not deal with each other at all."

"Yea and they turn out fucked up."

"I didn't." I said.

"Aight. You trippin." he said.

"Whatever. I'm about to go. Ava will be with my mom this weekend, if you want to see her."

Nia Rich

CHANEL

Chapter 6

We were fresh off the honeymoon, and I was back home with my new husband. I was so happy with everything in my life, and I hadn't stopped smiling since the wedding day. The wedding was as beautiful as I imagined it to be, and the honeymoon was even better. I couldn't wait to get back to work, so I could tell everyone who couldn't make it to the wedding about the entire experience. I put my luggage by our bed, opened it, and started putting my things away. Orlando put his bags down and walked over to me.

He wrapped his arms around my waist and said, "I know you don't think I am going to let you do anything before I make love to my wife for the first time in our house."

I giggled and turned to face him. I wrapped my arms around his neck and kissed him. We walked backwards a few steps while kissing until we reached the bed. He laid me down and then he took off his t shirt. My eyes scanned his tall, tattoo free, muscular frame. When he took off his jeans, my eyes went straight to his tool poking through his boxers. I smiled and started taking my shirt and shorts off, and then I went straight for his tool. I put it in my mouth and bobbed my head up and down on it. He moaned and tilted his head back. I took it out of my mouth and gave his jewels a few licks, and then I put it back into my mouth.

"Oooo shit." he moaned as I started bobbing my head up and down on it again.

He said, "Turn over and get on your knees."

I turned over and got on my knees as he asked. He put his tool inside of me and started giving me the business. I gripped the comforter on our bed to keep my balance. I looked back at him while he put it down on me.

"Mmmm. Orlando. I love you." I moaned.

"I love you too wife. This mine forever. You hear me?"

"Yeeeessss." I moaned. I had a fast orgasm. He always made me do that. My knees buckled so I laid flat onto my stomach. Orlando didn't miss a beat. He kept at it. He switched speeds a few times, he squeezed my ass, he leaned down and kissed my back and shoulders, and then he flipped me over. He kissed me some more, he sucked on my nipples, he used one of his hands to put a little pressure on my lower belly while he continued to pump in and out of me, and then he grunted and busted inside of me. After he pulled out, he laid on the bed next to me and smiled.

"This is a good start of the first day home as husband and wife." he said.

I said, "Yes, it is."

"Are you going to make your husband something to eat."

"Yup. After we put our things away."

"Aight. Come take a shower with me." he said.

I smiled, kissed him, and then I followed him to the bathroom.

***

After we finished our shower together, I decided to put our things away before cooking the lunch he requested. Orlando had gone downstairs to take a phone call from one of his friends. I could hear him telling his friend about the honeymoon. I finished putting my things away, and then I threw his luggage on the bed, and started putting his clothes away. I threw his dirty clothes in a hamper, and then I walked back over to the open suitcase to finish putting his clean clothes up. When I reached back into the luggage to grab more stuff, I noticed a black box with gold letters sticking out from the luggage pocket. I reached and pulled out the magnum condom box. I looked in it. There was only one condom left in it. I frowned. *What the fuck?* I thought.

I turned on my heels and stormed out of the room with the box of condoms in hand. I found him standing in the kitchen with his back up against the island counter and a glass of Hennessey in his hand. He was talking to his friend through his Blue Tooth device connected to his phone. I walked right up to him and put the box of condoms in his face.

"What the hell is this?" I asked with much attitude.

Orlando paused and put his drink on the counter, he said, "Aye man let me call you back."

I stood there with my face screwed waiting for an answer.

He nonchalantly took the box of condoms out of my hand and asked, "Where did you get this?"

"From your luggage Orlando! There is only one left!" I yelled.

"Baby calm down. I didn't know that these were in there. They have probably been in there since before I met you. I haven't carried that luggage in a while. I usually travel with a duffle bag and a carry on."

I sucked my teeth, crossed my arms under my breasts, and rolled my eyes to the ceiling.

"Baby I'm serious."

"I don't want to be going through this with you Orlando."

"Baby you're not. I promise." he said, and then he put the box on the counter behind him and said, "Come here. I love you. You don't have to worry about nothing like that. Ok?"

He pulled me into his arms and hugged me. I melted into his embrace, and then I responded, "Ok."

"Now, how about that lunch you promised me?" Orlando asked.

"I didn't promise you anything." I said.

"Yes, you did. While I was beating that thang up." he said.

I laughed and pushed him away from me. "Ok. I'll take care of you hubby."

I walked away and started pulling things out of the refrigerator and cabinets to cook. That box of condoms was the red flag that I should've been paying attention to. It was our first day home from our honeymoon. Only three days into our marriage and my man might have already cheated on me. My gut was telling me that I had possibly made the biggest mistake of my life marrying Orlando, but I pushed the box of condoms to the back of my mind and prepared my new husband a meal for lunch.

Chapter 7

A few hours later, we were lying on the couch watching television together. Orlando's phone started ringing, so he answered it.

"Sup bro? Yea I am back. Aight cool." he hung up and looked at me. "That was Donte babe he wants me to come through."

"Babe we just got back. Don't you want to relax with your wife and enjoy being married?"

"I do baby, but Donte wants to show me something."

"He can't show you another time?"

"Baby. I'll be back, and then we can lay up all night and then all day tomorrow.

I exhaled and rolled my eyes. "Alright. Don't be too late."

"I won't baby I promise." he said, and then he kissed me.

After he left, I picked up my phone and called Melanie. If I was going to be home for a few hours, I was going to get a little girl chat in. Melanie answered the phone quickly.

"Hey wifey!" she yelled into the phone.

"Hi honey." I said.

"How is everything in married land? Are you two back home now?

"Yes. We made it back today and I am already home alone."

"Really?"

"Yes. He ran off with Donte somewhere."

"Well. You know how those two are when they are together. It's like they are joined at the hip sometimes."

"I know and now I am here by myself."

"You better get used to it because that is how it's going to be when the season starts back up."

I sighed. "I know." I said.

"Well, don't fret. I will be in town in a couple of weeks, so we can hang out."

"Alright."

After the phone call, I took a bath, and did a few things around the house. When I was finished, I laid down in bed, and then I turned on the television. I had to be back to work in a couple weeks, so I wanted to enjoy relaxing. I was hoping to spend most of that time with my husband. Somewhere between the first and the second show I fell asleep. When I woke up, it was three o'clock in the morning, but Orlando was not there.

I turned over while still sleep and touched his side of the bed, and that is when I realized that I was in bed alone. His side of the bed was cold, so I opened my eyes and looked around our room. The whole house was dark except for the plug-in nightlights in the hallways. I sat up in the bed and picked up my phone. I had no missed calls from Orlando. I rubbed my eyes, located his number in my phone, and tapped the screen to call him. His phone rang straight to voicemail, so I sent him a text asking him where he was. I set the phone on the nightstand and got up to use the bathroom. When I was finished in the bathroom, I got back into bed, turned the television back on, and then my phone started ringing. It was Orlando returning my call.

"Where are you?" I asked.

"Baby I know. I'm sorry, and I am on my way." he responded.

"It is almost four in the morning Orlando." I said angrily.

"I know. I know. I apologize. I will be there soon."

I put my phone back down and watched my television until he arrived. I heard the garage door twenty minutes later, and Orlando came jogging upstairs. He walked right over to me and dove on top of me.

"Baby I'm sorry." he said as he hugged me. He started placing kisses all over my face. I could smell liquor on his breath, so I knew they'd probably been to the club. Knowing Orlando and Donte, it was probably a strip club.

"Stop Orlando. I am mad at you." I said.

He stopped kissing me to say, "Baby I know, and I didn't mean to come home this late. Me and Donte got carried away and time got away from us."

"Yea, but you left your new wife home all day and night. That is not cool Orlando."

He started squeezing me in a tight hug. "I know baby and I am sorry. Please forgive me. I won't do it again."

I let him kiss me, and then I rolled my eyes and said, "Alright. I forgive you."

He smiled and said, "That's my baby."

He kissed me and the he reached down to touch my peach. I said, "Uh-Uh. Not before you take shower." I pointed towards the bathroom.

He chuckled and stood up. "Aight. Be naked when I come back." Orlando said.

I did exactly what he said. I got naked and waited for him to come back to bed. He came back to bed a few minutes later with just a towel wrapped around his waist. I was instantly turned on when I saw his body. I crawled across the bed to him, touched his muscular chest, and then

I started placing kisses on his belly. I stopped to pull his towel off. I put my hand on his stiff tool, put it in my mouth, and began bobbing my head up and down on it. He groaned, and then he tilted his head back. I used my hand to rub his tool while I bobbed my head up and down on him.

He let me go to work on him for a while and then he said, "Lay down."

I backed up and laid on to my back. He spread my legs open and put his face in between. When I felt his lips on my lotus blossom, I purred, "Oooo."

"Mmm hmm." he moaned.

I held my legs open while he kissed, licked, and sucked on my gem. When I got wet, he stood up and pushed his tool inside of me. Orlando grabbed my legs, pushed them back, and then he pounded into me. I grabbed the sheets, an then I made a few loud sounds, but not too loud and not too ratchet. I kept my moans sweet and cute. He smacked my butt, and then spread my legs open wide. I loved it when he put me in airplane position.

"Yes babe." I moaned.

"That's what you like ain't it?"

"Yes. stay right there." I said.

He stayed on my spot and pounded relentlessly until my orgasm hit me. I let out a high pitch sigh, and then my body shivered. When he felt my waterfall, he started going even harder until he got his. He grunted when he busted, and then he pulled out and let it go on my stomach.

After he finished, he said, "Come on let's go and take a shower.

Chapter 8

I took a picture of all the new designer bags and shoes Orlando had bought for me. I posted the picture on my social media page, and then I sent the picture to Adara with a caption that read, "I love him."

I smiled, and then I picked up one of the designer purses and modeled it in the mirror.

"It looks good on you babe."

"Thank you. I love all of this."

"Do you forgive me?"

"Yes, I do." I said. I turned around and hugged him

"Which one are you going to wear tonight?" he asked.

"I am going to wear these leopard Gucci pumps and this Gucci bag."

"You gonna be killing em babe." Orlando said.

"Yes I am. I should start getting dressed now."

"Yea because it takes you like five hours to get dressed."

"Be quiet. No, it doesn't." I said.

"Let you tell it. I'll be downstairs waiting for you." Orlando said, and then he kissed me, smacked me on the butt, and left the room.

***

"It's the newlyweds!" Orlando's friend Travis said when he opened the door to his home.

"Sup bro! Happy birthday!" Orlando said before slapping hands with him. Travis's wife walked up to me and gave me a hug.

"Girl you look great. I love these shoes." Lisa said.

"Thank you. Compliments of my husband."

"You got taste Orlando." Lisa said as we walked through the house to where Travis's birthday party was being held.

There was a DJ, a bunch of players, and their wives at the party. Me and Orlando made our rounds greeting people, and then we made our way to the food platter in the kitchen.

"Help yourself to everything." Travis said.

We got a little food and some drink, and then we mixed in with the party. I ended up by a few of the wives; including Lisa. Orlando walked over and stood near the guys to chat. The wives were talking about some girl that one of the other wives had brought to the party. From the sounds of it, they didn't like her, and they were throwing major shade. Especially the lady of the house.

"I don't even know why she brought that bitch here anyways." Lisa said. Lisa is bi-racial. She is African American and Caucasian. She has long, brown curly hair. She is skinny, tall, and has fake breasts and booty. I met her during a double date we had with her and her husband Travis. We hit it off well, so we stayed in touch.

"I don't know either. You know she has made her way around the league." One of the other women said. She was, slim, tall, and light brown. She was wearing a long weave with a part in the middle, and she had extremely long hot pink nails.

"You know she is a known side chick." Another woman said. She was the color of caramel. She was short, thick, had a flat stomach, and a shoulder tattoo. She was wearing her hair in a long ponytail.

"I know one thing, she better stay away from my husband." Lisa said.

"Who are y'all talking about?" I asked.

"That bitch with the bum ass, bleach blonde, lace front." The woman with the long hair parted down the middle said. The group of women started laughing. I looked over at the girl they were talking about. I had never seen her before, but she was dressed like she wanted some attention at a party that had mostly couples there.

"You better watch her." Lisa warned.

"Yea that bitch ain't shit." The woman with the long hair said.

"Anyways girl let me introduce you to everyone. This is, Tami, Letisha, and Kamira."

"Hi. I am Chanel."

"This is Orlando's new wife." Lisa said.

"Oh ok. You're pretty. My husband told me that Orlando got married, but I didn't believe it. I had to see it with my own eyes." Letisha said. She was the one with the long hair. She flicked her long hair over her shoulder. "Well congratulations. I thought you were just one of his weekend things. No disrespect, but he was always showing up with someone new."

"Shut up girl." Lisa said.

"What? I'm just saying. I'm glad somebody finally settled his ass down." Letisha said.

"Anyways. Excuse my best friend. Congrats girl." Lisa said. The other women replied the same.

"Thank you." I replied.

"Can I see your ring girl?" Tami asked. She was the one with the shoulder tattoo.

Kamira walked over to see it too. "This is gorgeous." she said. She had a light brown complexion like

Lisa. She was my height and she was wearing her hair wavy with a side part.

"Thank you." I said.

"So, what are you going to do when the season starts?" Tami asked.

"I'll be working." I said.

"You have a job?" Tami asked.

"Yes. I work for a magazine." I responded.

"That is cool." Kamira said.

"My husband won't let me work. He wants me home with our kids." Letisha said.

"I've never had a job. I met my husband while I was trying to get my modeling career started." Tami said.

"I was an exotic dancer when I met mine. I went from a pole to a palace." Kamira said.

"And you still got a pole in your house." Letisha said.

"Hey, you can take the me out of the strip club, but you can't take the stripper out of me." Kamira said.

"Geesh." Tami said.

"Be quiet. My husband loves it. All y'all need a little stripper in your lives. I can teach you if you want to learn." Kamira said.

"As you can see, they are all crazy. If you need something to do or you just want to chill, call me anytime girl. We are always hanging out during the season." Lisa said.

"Alright thanks."

"Uh-uh." Lisa said as she looked across the room. The girl they had been talking about was talking to Orlando. She was laughing and giggling, and Orlando was being his normal charming self.

"I suggest that you go and get your man away from that thirsty hoe." Letisha said as she was looking that way too.

I excused myself from the ladies and walked across the room to where they were standing.

"Hello." I said.

"Hi. You must be the wife. He was just telling me about you. You are very beautiful." she said with a huge smile.

"Thanks. Can I talk to him for a second, please?"

"Oh absolutely. It was great meeting you Orlando."

He smiled and said, "Likewise."

After she walked away, I said, "I am ready to go."

"Alright" he said. He walked over and slapped hands with his boys. I went back over to hug the ladies and then we left.

Chapter 9

Melanie and I got together to go shopping a couple of weeks later. She was my only friend who visited New York frequently. She was chasing a career in fashion, so she traveled a lot. Plus, she was dating a ball player that lived there. I loved having my best friend around; especially since I didn't have my sister Adara around. We decided to stop through Soho for some quality shopping. I had to go back to work the next day and I needed to be up to date on everything fashion. Melanie and I decided to hit up a few of my favorites first. Chanel, Gucci, and Louis Vuitton. I was standing outside looking up and down the block of tan brick buildings with all my favorite stores lined in a row searching for Melanie. She said that she would meet me in front of the Chanel store.

"Hi wifey!" Melanie said when she walked up.

She had her wavy hair pulled back into a ponytail with a pair of designer shades on. Her skin had the perfect tan like she had just been kissed by the sun. I was sure that she'd been spray tanning recently. She has the same light skin complexion as Adara, but she is a Miami native and loves to look bronzed like she'd been tanning all day.

I smiled and said, "Hi!"

"Look at you. You're still glowing."

"You think so?"

"Yes. You look gorgeous."

I said, "Thank you." I moved my bangs across my forehead to the left side. I always wear my hair parted to the left. I feel like my right side is my best side. I was rocking a pair of Chanel shades and carrying a Chanel bag.

Melanie said, "I see your dressed in your favorite designer."

I said, "Of course darling. It is my mom's favorite designer and that is how I got the name."

"I know, and you look good in it." she said.

"Thank you. I love those Christian Louboutin's that you have on."

"Yes, they're the classic nude patent leather pumps."

"I know! I've been wanting to get my hands on those."

"I think that I found them at Saks." she said as we turned to walk into the store.

"They are my favorite, and you look stunning as usual darling." I said. I examined the Louis Vuitton bag she was carrying, and then I smiled at the door guy holding the door for us to walk into the exquisite retail store. It was like walking into retail heaven upon entering the store. I looked around at all the designer items that I needed to get my hands on.

"What's been up wifey?" she asked.

"Been preparing to go back to work. I'm not ready. I could use another week."

"I hear you. I don't think anyone is ever ready to go back to work."

"No, and especially not when you have to deal with a bitch for a boss like mine."

"I know. I couldn't deal with her. I would've smacked her in the face and quit." she said.

I laughed and said, "Trust me, I've thought about it a time or two." I picked up a shoe and looked at it. "I like this." I said.

"Me too." So, tell me about married life. How has it been?" Melanie asked.

I put the shoes down and we walked towards some hand bags. "It has been amazing." I responded as picked up a handbag and examined it.

"I know it has girl. I am so happy for you. You are a married woman now. I'll be glad when someone finally puts a ring on my finger."

I laughed, and then I said, "I met some of the other wives."

"When?"

"A couple of weeks ago at Travis's birthday party. You know who Travis is, right?"

"Yes. He plays for the same team as Orlando."

"Yup. It was his wife and a few of her friends."

"What were they like?"

"Travis's wife, Lisa was cool. Her friends were a bit much. Especially Letisha. She has a lot of mouth."

Melanie laughed. "You're a part of the wives' club now. You better get used to it because you're going to be seeing a lot of them."

I put the bag I was holding down and picked up another one. "I have a question." I said.

"Shoot." she responded.

"How would you feel if you found a pack of condoms in your man's luggage the day after your honeymoon?"

Melanie paused. "What?" she asked.

"Yes."

She put the bag that she was holding down and turned to face me.

"Are you trying to tell me that your brand-new husband cheated on you right after the wedding?"

"I think that he did. There was only one condom left in the box."

"Oh my gosh." she said, and then she shook her head back and forth.

"I know, and I don't know how to feel about it."

"See that is that bullshit. How dare he do that?"

"I don't know. He claims that it was an old box that had been in his luggage for a while."

"Do you believe him?

"Part of me does and part of me doesn't. I feel like damn if he did, how disrespectful to do it right after our wedding."

"Dang that is not cool girl. I hope he is not lying to you. It's too early in the game to be doing stuff like that."

"I know right." I said as I picked up another bag and modeled it in the mirror.

"I like this" I said. I was holding a small cream and black colored hobo bag.

"Yea that is cute. I really like the cream-colored tweed." she said.

"I do too." I said.

"I think I am going to get this silver one on my boo." she said.

"Oh, you got his card today?"

"You know it." Melanie smiled.

"I am going to get this one." I said. We started walking towards the register with the three thousand-dollar bags in our hands.

"On top of that, he stayed out until four o'clock in the morning the first night we were home."

"No." she said.

"Yes, girl I was pissed, but he bought me a bunch of designer shoes and bags to make up for it."

"Well, a little Gucci does help get over stuff."

I laughed and said, "Stop it."

"I'm just saying."

"You have a point. I did forgive him for staying out late."

"So, what are you going to do about that situation with the condoms." she asked.

"I don't have no proof that it is a recent box of condoms, so I am just going to relax and enjoy being newlyweds."

"I hear you. We should stop by a nail salon. These nails are done." she said.

I looked at my French manicured nails. "I could use a refill and some new polish. Let's go after we stop in the Gucci store."

"Yes, let's do that." she said.

We paid for our new Chanel bags and left the store.

Chapter 10

I made it back home a few hours later. I walked in the house with bags from my shopping trip with Melanie. In addition to the designer handbags that I bought, I got my nails and toes done, and picked up a sexy lingerie outfit to wear for Orlando. I planned to cook and spend a nice evening with my new husband, and then make love to him all night. However, Orlando had other plans.

Before I could get all the way in the house, he met me at the door and said, "Hey baby. I'm about to get up with Donte and Trav. I'll be back."

I gave him a disappointed look and said, "I was going to cook for us babe."

"I know. You can still cook for us babe. I'm going to be back."

"Are you going to be out late again Orlando?"

"No babe. I promise. I'll be back. Ok?"

He caught me off guard, and the only thing I could say was, "Ok."

Orlando kissed me, and then he walked out of the garage door. I gloomily walked up the stairs to our bedroom, put my shopping bags down, and plopped down on the bed. I wished that I would have hung out with Melanie a little longer or invited her over. If I would have known that Orlando was going to leave me at home alone again, I would have. I called her to see what she was doing, but she didn't answer the phone. Earlier that day she had told me that she was going to spend time with her boyfriend when we finished our day out. I knew that she was probably with him. I disconnected the call when I heard her voicemail pick up. I dropped the phone on the bed, stood up, and walked back down the stairs to the kitchen to start preparing dinner.

***

I was sitting at our kitchen table with my lingerie on, candles lit, food prepared, and a glass of wine in my hand. I was on my second glass of wine and Orlando hadn't made it home yet. It was close to eleven o'clock at night and he had been gone all day. I thought he would've been home before midnight since he had promised. I picked up my phone and scrolled through my social media page while I waited. Time was going by fast and before I knew it, it was fifteen minutes to midnight, the food was cold, and there was no sign of Orlando. I decided to call him. The phone rang a couple of times, and then he answered. I could hear loud music and a lot of loud talking in his background.

"Hey baby what's up?" he yelled over the music.

"Where are you?" I asked.

"I am still with Donte and Trav. I will be home soon."

"Soon when? You told me that you wouldn't be out late tonight babe."

"I know, and I am not."

"It's already midnight."

"I know baby, but I am leaving soon. I promise."

"The food is cold now babe."

"I'm sorry. We can reheat it when I get home. I will be there." he said, and then I heard Donte saying something in the background. "I got to go baby. I will be there soon."

He hung up and I set my phone down on the counter and started putting everything away. I was disappointed. I had put in all that work to have a special evening with my new husband and he ruined it to be out with his friends.

After I was done cleaning the kitchen, I changed out of my lingerie, and put on a satin pajama set. I made a bowl of fruit, sat on the couch, and turned on the television. An hour went by, and then two, and then three. I had called him multiple times and he told me he was coming every time he answered the phone. I was irritated and trying to stay calm, but I was ready to go off on him. Orlando didn't waltz his ass back into the house until four o'clock in the morning again. By that time, I had gone from irritated to being extremely angry with him.

I was awake and still on the couch, when he made it home. I was lying on my back scrolling through my social media pages on my phone. The television was on, but it was watching me. He walked in through the garage door and walked straight to the living room where I was.

"Hey baby." he said.

"It's four o'clock in the morning again Orlando." I said angrily without looking up from my phone.

"I know, but-"

I cut him off. "I don't even want to hear your explanation. You promised me that you would be home early tonight."

"I know baby, but you know how it is when I am with Donte and Trav. Time gets away from us sometimes."

"Yea, but we just got married, and I was looking forward to spending some time with my new husband before returning to work tomorrow morning."

He put his hand on his forehead and said, "Oh damn, baby I forgot. I'm sorry."

"I'm going to bed. Good night."

I stood up and walked back through the house and up the stairs to our room. I slammed out bedroom door shut. He stayed in the living room for a while, and then I heard him walk into our room when the sun was coming up. He kissed me a couple of times to try to wake me up. I wasn't completely asleep because I was still fuming, but I ignored him. He climbed in bed and curled up next to me. When he saw that I wasn't responding to him, he turned over and went to sleep.

Chapter 11

The next days, I walked into the kitchen and put my keys on the counter. I had just made it home from my first day of work. My head was pounding, my feet were hurting, and I had a ton of things to get done for work. I picked up the mail on the counter and began flipping through each envelope to see if anything came for me. Orlando walked around the counter with a glass of orange juice in hand.

"Hey baby." he said before taking another sip from his orange juice.

"Hey." I said. I put the mail back down on the counter.

"Are you still mad about last night?" he asked, and then he took another sip from his orange juice.

I folded my arms over my chest and looked at him. "I am."

"I apologize baby. I got carried away with the guys."

"I had a whole night planned for us babe and you ruined it." I said.

"I know, and I am sorry baby. Let me make it up to you." he said.

He pulled a long box out of his pocket and handed it to me. I looked at it, closed my eyes, and then I smiled. I took the box from him and opened it. There was a diamond bracelet inside.

"Thank you, babe." I said.

"Do you like it?" he asked.

"I love it."

"I thought you would." he said as he removed the bracelet from the box and put it on my wrist. I held my arm out to look at the sparkling diamonds.

"Do you forgive me?" he asked.

"Yes, I do." I said. I turned to hug him. He wrapped his arms around me and squeezed me. After we shared a kiss, he asked, "How was your first day back to work?"

"It was absolute craziness. Everyone was happy to see me back, but it was extremely busy, I had a bunch of meetings, and my boss was a complete bitch." I said as I removed my Christian Louboutin's from my feet. "My head is hurting, and my feet are killing me."

"Aww baby. I am sorry."

"It's alright. It comes with the job."

"Come here baby." Orlando said.

He pulled me into his arms. His warm, muscular body felt good up against mine. My face rested on his chest as he hugged me. "I missed you today. I was thinking baby. I don't want my wife working. I want you home with me."

"Awww baby. That is sweet." I said.

"I'm serious." he said. He lightly pushed me away from him, so he could look me in the eyes. "Baby, I know that you like to make your own money, and that is one of the reasons that I love you so much, but you don't have to worry about all that. I got us. I want you home with me being my wife. I don't want you working, tired, and stressing over no bitch ass boss and all that. I want you home, peaceful, and beautiful like you are."

"Babe I like working. Fashion is my life. That is what I do."

"I know baby. Your fashion game is on point, and there are so many other things that you can do with fashion these days from home. You can start your own fashion blog, and pod cast. I can even invest in an online boutique for you, if you want to have your own business. You don't need a boss. You are the boss. It's time to boss up baby and live this boss life with me. You feel me?" he said.

I laughed, and then I asked, "Boss up?"

"Yes. Do you see my vision?" he asked.

"I can see your vision baby." I said and smiled. "What about when the season starts again? I am going to be here by myself and bored while you're busy all day."

"No, you're not. You'll be busy starting your business's and hanging out with the other wives."

"I don't know about that."

He chuckled and said, "They will grow on you."

"Let you tell it." I said.

"So, what's up? Are you putting in your two weeks or what?"

"Yes, baby, I am."

He smiled. "Aight. Cool." he kissed me and said, "What are you hooking up for dinner, or do you want to go out?"

"Can we go out baby please?"

"Yup. You pick the place. I am going to get dressed."

Nia Rich

ADARA

Chapter 12

Holding my daughters' bottle of milk in my hand, I walked from the kitchen to her room and put it in her hands. I picked her up and laid her down in her crib, put her blanket over her, and then I walked quietly out of her room and clicked off the light. I sat down on my couch and picked up my phone. I had a text message. I smiled when I saw that is was from Dr. Miles Nash.

Hi beautiful. I hope that you had a good day.

I smiled and sent him a reply.

Thank you. I did. I hope that you did too.

I sent mine with a smiley face emoji and set my phone next to me. After meeting him at the wedding, he was sending me sweet texts like that every day. Some nights we were on the phone talking until late night, after he put his daughter to bed. I was enjoying his attention, but I wasn't sure if I was ready to be moving forward with a new man. He told me that he understood where I was at and that he was alright with building a friendship. I liked that he lived out of state because it was easier to focus on a friendship and not rush into anything. He responded to my text and told me that he would call me later, and then my phone started ringing. I rolled my eyes before answering it.

"Hello." I said dryly.

Wes said, "Adara."

"Yes?"

"Where is my princess?"

"I just laid her down to sleep."

"How was she today?"

"She was fine."

"Um, my cousin is having a kick back this weekend at his crib. I was hoping that you would bring my daughter. My family will be in town and they would be happy to see you and her. It's not going to be nothing ghetto. It is a family affair."

"I don't know Wes."

"Come on Adara. Don't be like that. My family wants to see you and our daughter. Can we please put our differences aside just this one time? For the family and for our daughter?"

"I'm just not trying to be around you, if you're going to be drinking."

"Adara I know, and I promise I will not be drinking. My mom is going to be there."

I sighed loudly, I paused before saying, "Ok Wes. I will bring Ava."

"Thank you Adara." Wes said. I could tell that he was smiling.

I rolled my eyes again and said, "Alright. I have to go."

"Ok. It is Saturday at two at my cousins. You remember where he lives, right?"

"Yup."

"Alright. I'll see you there."

We disconnected the call. He was lucky that my shop was going to be closed that Saturday for renovations, or I would have said no. I was getting the shops walls repainted, and the floors redone. We had so many color spills on my floors, they were starting to look like an abstract painting.

Since breaking up with Wes, I'd gotten my finances back in order. I was focused on my shop and not Wes, and it felt good to have things back in order. My phone started ringing a few minutes later. I answered it when I saw Miles's name flash across the screen.

"Hello."

"Hi beautiful."

I smiled and said, "Hi."

"How was your day?" he asked.

"It was alright. I didn't have too many clients, so I didn't work that hard."

"That is good."

"How was yours?"

"I had a long day today, so I am glad to be home and relaxing. It's good to hear your voice after a long day though."

I smiled and said, "It's good to hear yours too."

"Is your daughter sleep?"

"Yes. Yours?"

"Yes. Finally. She tried to run me ragged when I picked her up from the sitter."

I laughed and said, "Ava tries to do the same to me when I pick her up from my mom. Her dad's family is in town and I am taking her to see them and I don't know how I feel about it."

"Think positive. I am sure they will be happy to see you and her. They don't have anything to do with what you are going through with him."

"That's true. Well, I need to get into bed, or I am going to be no good in the salon tomorrow."

"Me too. It was good hearing your voice. How about video chat tomorrow?"

"Ok."

"Great. I will see you then."

I smiled and hung up the phone.

Chapter 13

When I walked into Wes's cousin's backyard, Wes's mom's face lit up.

"Hey Suga!" she said. She walked over to me, hugged me, kissed me on the cheek, and then she grabbed Ava out of my arms.

"Look at my grandbaby! She has gotten so big and pretty!" she said.

She started kissing Ava on the cheeks, and then the rest of the family gathered around to great me and Ava. I can't lie, I am happy to see all of them. I wasn't so enthused about seeing Wes, but he was the last person in line to greet me.

"Hi Adara." he said.

He looked as good as the last time I saw him a year ago. Still chocolate, still muscular, still fine. He had his hair faded with a full beard.

"Hello." I said back. He opened his arms for a hug. I could feel eyes on us, so I accepted his hug.

"It's good to see you. You look good." he said.

"You do too. I see you've grown out your beard."

"Yea trying something new."

I said, "It's trending right now."

"I know. Our daughter looks beautiful. I meant to tell you that you are doing a great job with her."

"Thank you, but you don't have to lay it on so thick. I know that you're trying to get back in my good graces." I said.

He laughed and said, "I'm serious though."

I broke eye contact with him to locate our daughter. Her grandmother was still holding her. I looked around the backyard. There were a bunch of plastic chairs set up out there.

"Have a seat. I will make you a plate. We have lots of food."

I wanted to tell him that I would make my own plate, but I didn't want to be a jerk in front of his family. I walked through the backyard and found a seat next to his mom. I watched the family pass Ava around while Wes made my plate. He was on his best behavior. Being all well-mannered and stuff. Looking and smelling all good. He thought he was slick. Trying to show off in front of his family.

Uuugh I can't stand his ass. I thought.

He came back with the plate of food he made, handed it to me, and then he found an empty chair next to me. We sat around talking and laughing with his family for a while. They told me a few stories about him as a child like they always do. They doted over how Ava looks just like the both of us. It felt like old times. Wes did not have one drink. He was completely sober, and he wasn't even high off weed. I wasn't impressed, but I was happy that he kept his word.

After a couple of hours, I stood up to go and make a plate of food to take home as Wes's cousin instructed. Wes walked into the kitchen a few minutes after me.

"Can I talk to you for a second?" Wes asked.

I sighed, and then I said, "Sure."

"Let's go in here."

I followed him to the living room. We sat down on the couch.

"I know that you don't fuck with me no more and that's cool. The truth is, I understand. A nigga is a fuck up. I know, and I can't change what I have done, but I just want to come by sometime and see my daughter. Is that too much to ask?"

I sighed again. "I don't know Wes."

"You got to at least give me that. I'm trying to be in her life."

"Alright. We'll work out a schedule.

He smiled. "Cool thank you."

"You're welcome."

"Well I don't want to hold you up. I know you got to get Ava home."

Wes helped me pack some food, get Ava's diaper bag, and after I kissed and hugged the family, he walked me and Ava to the car. He helped me strap her into the car seat, he kissed her, and then he stood on the side walk until we pulled off.

Chapter 14

I was standing behind my stylist chair putting curls in Nikita's hair. I was trying to get her finished before my next client showed up. It was a busy Saturday at the salon. Bianca, Kyra and Deon all had clients in their chairs. Deon had clients lined up for haircuts. Nikita was being chatty as usual. I was tired, but I was still talking with her even though I didn't feel like it. Nikita asked me how the family barbeque was at Wes's house.

"It was fine girl. His family was extremely happy to see me and Ava."

"How did you feel when you saw Wes?"

"I had mixed feelings. He was on his best behavior though."

"Girl you know you wanted to get that thang tapped when you saw him."

I laughed. "Absolutely not. I'm not thinking about Wes."

"Um hum. Well, anyways girl. I've been talking to that one baller that I did my thing with in New York."

"I thought that was supposed to be a one-night thing."

"It was, but he found me on social media. I guess I put it on him."

"I heard that." Deon said loudly from across the salon.

Nikita laughed, and then I said, "It's that big ass you got cousin."

"I admit, my twerk game is on point."

"You know that I know, and so does everyone who saw it on the dance floor at the wedding."

Nikita laughed again and said, "He is talking about flying me out to Chicago. That is who he plays for."

"What are y'all talking about? Bianca asked from her station.

"That little cutie I met at the wedding." Nikita replied.

"Do you have a picture of him?" Bianca asked.

"Yup." Nikita said as I finished the last few curls in her hair. She scrolled through pictures in her phone until she found the picture them.

"You kept the picture from the wedding in your phone?" I asked as I sprayed oil sheen on her hair. A cloud of mist surrounded her head. After the mist settled, I sprayed some hairspray, and then I picked through the curls with a rat tail comb. When I finished, I handed Nikita a mirror. I turned the swivel backwards, so she could use the mirror to see the back of her hair.

"Yes cousin. This is perfect. I like that new design you did back there. Thank you."

"Not a problem. You know that I always got you."

Nikita stood up and walked over to Bianca's station to show her a picture of the ball player.

"Oh yea. He is fine. Doesn't he play for Chicago?"

"Yup." Nikita said.

"Let me see." Kyra said.

"How did you snag that?" Bianca asked.

"Twerking." I said.

Everyone in the salon laughed.

"Shut up cousin." Nikita said.

"For real." I said.

"Dang. You must have been doing your thing?" Bianca said.

"Let's see your twerk game now." Deon said.

"No." Nikita said bashfully.

"Uh huh." Deon said.

He picked up the radio remote and turned up the volume. People in the salon started chanting and encouraging her to do it. Nikita stood up, bent over, and started shaking and bouncing her butt. She put on a whole twerk show for the salon. Deon, Bianca, and a couple of our clients dropped dollar bills on her. She looked like a girl from one of the videos I've seen on my social media pages. When she finished, the salon cheered for her. She picked up the money people threw at her and said, "Thanks. I am about to buy my son some lunch."

Deon said, "I see why dude was hitting you up. With all that ass twerking like that I would have hit you up too."

The salon erupted in laughter. I watched Kyra step outside to take a phone call. I smiled when I read a text from Miles. I sent him a reply text and then, I sent a reply text to Wes telling him that he could some over the next day. I put my phone back into my pocket, and then I walked my cousin Nikita to the door. She said goodbye to everyone in the shop, gave me a hug, and told me that she would call me later.

Chapter 15

Wes showed up at my house the next day for the first-time after the break up. He walked in with flowers for me and bags of stuff for Ava. He hugged me, and I got a whiff of his cologne. His smell was enticing. He was wearing a brand-new pair of designer jeans, brand new all black sneakers, and a black polo style t-shirt. He was looking good, but I kept a cool demeanor. I couldn't let him know that I felt attracted to him. He took Ava from my arms and kissed her on the cheek. She started giggling. He complimented my new furniture and home décor as he walked through the house to the living room. He sat down on the love seat with Ava in his lap.

"How have you been?" he asked.

"I have been well." I said.

"Yea. Well, you look gorgeous as always."

"Thank you."

"Thanks for letting me stop by finally."

"You're welcome." I said. I turned my attention to the television. There was a marathon of the Kardashians show on television. I was getting caught up on all the episodes that I had missed. We sat there for a while in silence watching the television and watching Ava play with her toys in the middle of the floor.

He broke the silence and asked, "How are things going at the shop?"

"Things a been going tremendously well. I have had a boost in new clientele and product sales, so I am happy."

"That's good Adara. I am happy for you. Congrats. For real."

"Thank you." I said, and then we went back to sitting in silence. It felt awkward sitting there with him, so I asked, "Do you mind sitting with Ava for a minute, so I can run to the store?"

"Go ahead. I got her."

"Thanks. I'll be right back." I got up and picked up my purse and left.

***

As I walked through the grocery store, I pulled my phone out of my cell phone out of my purse and called Nikita.

"What are you doing?" I asked when she answered.

"Sitting here polishing my nails and watching television. Jakari took our son to see his cousins. What are you up to?"

"Walking through the grocery store. Wes is at my house girl."

"Hold up. What!?"

"Girl yes. He came over to visit Ava."

"Why aren't you there?"

"I asked him to watch Ava, so I could run to the grocery store. I needed to pick up some things for dinner tonight"

"Are you going to let him tap that?" she asked.

"Girl. no."

"You know you want to."

"That is all you think about, and no, I don't want to. He is looking good though."

"Looking good was never his problem." she said.

"True."

"You didn't miss him?"

"Of course, I did, but I know what is best for me."

"Maybe he has changed."

"Maybe. He isn't high or drunk. That is two times now that I have seen him completely sober."

"See. He might have turned over a new leaf. Unlike Jakari's ass. He is cheating on me again girl. I am over it."

"I am not trying to hear that, 'I am done with him,' speech either." I said.

"I am."

"No, you're not. You never are."

"Well, I am this time."

"Um hum cousin. I love you and I am at the register, so I am about to go."

"Oh, before you go. I am flying out to Chicago to see that baller. If Jakari asks for any reason, I am with you."

"Oh, my goodness cousin."

"What? If Jakari can do it, I can do it better."

I laughed and then I disconnected the call after telling her that I would talk to her later.

Chapter 16

I heard my phone ringing upstairs. I was getting the laundry out of the dryer. I picked Ava up and hurriedly walked up the stairs to answer the phone. I thought that it was Wes calling to tell me that he was going to be late. He was stopping by to watch Ava while I did some shopping with the girls. He was coming by every Sunday for a month, and it was working out for us. When I saw that it was a call from Chanel, I snatched the phone up quick. I hadn't heard from her since the wedding. I saw her posting a bunch of stuff with her new husband all the time. They were at spa's, parties, and different events. It looked like she was living the good life, and like she had made some new friends as well. I was glad to see her happy even though I didn't approve of who she was married to.

"Hello." I answered breathlessly.

"Dang did I catch you at a bad time sis?" she asked.

"Hey sis. No. I was downstairs doing laundry. I had to run up here with Ava on my hip to answer the phone. It's good to hear from you though How are you? How's the married life going for the newlyweds?"

"It's going great! I am so happy. We've been having a wonderful time."

"I see. Y'all have been all over social media. How was going back to work?"

"It was cool. Everyone was excited to see me and talk about the wedding except my bitch for a manager."

I laughed and said, "You always said that you didn't like her."

"I don't, but I don't have to deal with her anymore."

"What do you mean? You got another job?"

"No. I'm quit. My husband doesn't want me to work anymore."

"You quit your job?" I asked.

"Yes, I did."

"Wow Chanel."

"I know. Don't worry. He said that he wants me home, so we have come up with a few ideas for me to work from home. I am going to start a fashion blog and a pod cast."

"That is great, but that's not guaranteed cash in your hand or a check every couple of weeks. That is more like a hobby."

"Yes, but we are fine. We have enough money and everything we need. Plus, I have money saved."

"Well, you sound happy, so I am happy for you."

"Thanks sis! The season has started back up, so I've been with the wives a lot."

"I was wondering who those chicks where in your posts online."

Yea they are cool, and Melanie has been around a lot."

"I saw that too."

"That is enough about me. How are you?"

"I am fine. Ava is getting so big. Just wait until you see her. She is trying to talk. She has been saying mommy."

"Awww. I need to fly up there to come and visit. I need to see my niece."

"Yes, you do."

"I will in a couple of weeks."

"Ok."

"What else is going on. Have you talk to my friend that I introduced you too?"

"Yes girl. We talk every day. I really like him."

"I knew that you would. He is a great person. Do I hear a love connection?"

"I don't know about all that, but I do enjoy talking to him."

"How are things with Wes?"

"Um. We have worked out a visitation schedule. He comes every Sunday to spend time with Ava, so I can run some errands."

"So, you two are talking now, and not going through your mom anymore."

"I guess you can say that."

"Uh oh."

"No. It's not what you think. At all. My mom and his mom were tired of being the middle women, so I decided to try to communicate and get along for the sake of Ava."

"Um hum. Well, I hope that he doesn't slither his way back in."

Adara laughed. "Hahaha! Slither? Stop it sister. Nobody is getting back in anywhere over here. He can be the daddy to Ava that he should be, and that is it."

"I hope so."

"I've got to go sister that is him at the door showing up for daddy duties."

"Ok I love you."

"I love you too. Let me know when you're coming up here."

"I will."

I hung up the phone with Chanel and walked to my front door to open it for Wes.

"Hey." I said when I opened the door.

"What's up lady." Wes said. He hugged me and then he took Ava from my arms. "Hey daddy's baby." he said. He started play biting her on her cheeks to make her laugh. It's something they do every time they see each other. Ava started cracking up laughing. I smiled and stepped back so he could walk in.

"How are you?" Wes asked as he was looking at Ava.

"I am fine. How are you?" I asked.

"I'm good." he said. He took some money out of his pocket and handed it to me.

"That is for you and Ava."

I put the stack of hundred-dollar bills in my pocket and said, "Thank you."

"No problem."

"Alright. I am out of here You know where everything is."

"Yup."

"Bye." I kissed Ava on the cheek and walked out of the door.

***

I met Nikita at the mall entrance.

"I invited Kyra to come. I hope that you don't mind." I said.

"Girl naw. Kyra is cool. I like her." Nikita replied.

"She said she is pulling in now."

We waited for Kyra to park and meet us at the entrance. She walked up rocking a floor length skirt and an off the shoulder top. The sunshine illuminated the sunflower tattoo on her shoulder. She smiled when she saw us. Her energy is always welcoming and positive.

"Hey beautiful ladies." she said when she walked up to us. She reached out to us both of us. She smelled like lavender oil and cocoa butter.

I said, "Hey beautiful," after I hugged her. "I love this skirt."

"Thank you." she responded.

"Yea girl. Your rocking that. For real." Nikita said.

"Thanks girl." she said as we walked into the mall.

We walked through the large hall; past the underground aquarium, the book store, and a chocolate store. We kept walking left.

"What store should we hit first?" I asked.

"Can we stop in Forever 21?" Nikita asked.

"Yea. I like that store." Kyra said.

"Ok." I said. We walked past a bunch of stores and then we headed into the enormous, two-level, clothing store.

"Where is Ava?" Kyra asked.

"She is with her dad." I said.

"Oh, That's good."

"How has that been going?" Nikita asked.

"It has been good. Ava absolutely loves her dad. You should see how she lights up when she sees him, and they have this special bond between them. It's so cute."

"Awww. I love that. I love seeing a man step up and do what he is supposed to do. You know? Because he could have just turned his back on her after you two broke up like a lot of these men do." Kyra said.

"You're right, and after what I've been through with him, I am very shocked to say the least."

"Are you fucking him yet?" Nikita asked.

"No girl." I replied.

Kyra laughed and said, "I'm surprised."

"Girl no. I am have not had sex since we broke up."

"Wait. You haven't had sex in over a year cousin?"

"No. I have a daughter. I am not trying to jump in the bed with any guy just because I get horny."

"I hear that." Kyra said.

"What about the doctor Chanel introduced you to?" Nikita asked.

"He is a really nice guy. He is a single dad. He works hard. I talk to him every day, but he lives out of state, so we haven't seen each other since the wedding. We just talk on the phone and video chat."

"That is good in my opinion. It gives you the chance to become friends first." Kyra said.

"I agree." I said.

"Girl please. I'ma need you to get that thang tapped. Ok?" Nikita said.

Me and Kyra laughed, and then I picked up a shirt and held it up, so they could see it.

"That is cute girl." Nikita said. "So, what's up with you Kyra. Do you have a man?"

"Yes, I do. He is on tour right now."

"On tour?"

"Yea. He is a DJ's for a famous rapper, and they are on tour right now for a few months."

"Illi-J's son, right?"

"Yup."

"Oh my gosh girl. The dude that has that song called, "Kissing Me", that is on the radio right now?" Nikita said.

"Yes."

"Oh wow. That is dope. Girl he is too fine. Why are you not on tour with him?"

"Oh no. I am not about that tour life. When he gets invited to do guest DJ gigs, I go with him sometimes, but that tour life is not for me. It messes with my energy."

I laughed. "I hear you."

"That has to be the shit dating a famous DJ." Nikita said.

"Yea. It comes with its perks, but it comes with its bullshit." Kyra said. She held up a dress and asked, "What do you think about this?"

"It's alright. I don't like that color." Nikita said.

"Yea. You're right." Kyra said. She put the dress back on the rack.

"Did being with him help you get your celebrity clients?" I asked.

"Yea it did because he introduced me to people, so it got my name out there. I like being at home, so my clients fly me out for big events like award shows and stuff like that, or when they are in town for concerts, they come to me or I go to them."

"That is hella cool." Nikita said.

"Well thank you." Kyra said. "Are you two hungry? I am."

"Let's go and get something to eat." I said.

We bought a few things from the store, and then we headed to one of the restaurants on the third floor to eat, drink, and have some more girl chat. After the waitress bought us glasses of wine, Nikita asked, "Have you talked to Chanel?"

"Yes, I talked to her today. I am still mad at her for marrying that fuck boy."

"His fine, rich ass." Nikita said.

"Girl please. I didn't even tell y'all that he tried to holla at me at the wedding."

"What?" Nikita asked.

Kyra's eyebrows went up. "No way." she said.

"Yea." I said.

"Did you tell her?" Kyra asked.

"No. I don't want to steal her joy and knowing her she is going to think that I am only saying it because I don't like him, and I am hating on her happiness."

"That's fucked up." Nikita said.

"Yea it is." Kyra said.

"It's not his first time trying to holla. I just didn't expect him to be fuck boy enough to do it at his own wedding. She doesn't know what she has gotten herself into, but she is going to have to learn on her own."

Chapter 17

Miles called me during my drive home from hanging with my girls. It always made me smile to hear his voice. We talked my entire ride home. He told me about his day, and a few things his daughter did that made him laugh. I told him about shopping and dinner with my girls. I told him that my baby was with her dad. I left out that he was at my house. When I pulled up to my house, we ended the conversation. I parked, got out of my car, and walked into the house. Wes was watching television, and Ava was asleep next to him.

"Aw. She fell asleep?" I asked quietly.

"Yea. I guess she got bored with me." he said.

I laughed, and then I gently picked Ava up and carried her to her room. After I laid her down in her bed, I walked back to the living room and said, "Thanks for watching her for me."

"She's my daughter. I wouldn't consider it watching her. I was spending time with her." he said as he stood up. I walked with him to the door, and then he asked, "Can I get a hug?"

"No." I responded.

"Why do you be acting like you don't miss me?" he asked.

"Because I don't." I said.

"I miss you."

"That's nice." I said. My text message notification went off, so I looked down at my phone.

"Who is that? Your new boyfriend?"

"No."

"Let me see."

"For what?"

"So, I can see who you have around my daughter."

"Nobody."

"Aight."

"I don't know why you are checking on me. I'm sure you have plenty of hoes to check on."

"No, I don't."

"Whatever Wes."

"Believe what you want. I don't. I've been waiting on you to realize that you still love me and give me another chance."

"I'm not trying to hear that. There isn't another chance, so it's time to move on."

"Is that what you are doing?"

"Yes, getting back to life."

"With who?"

"Why does there have to be somebody? I'm fine by myself. Me and my baby."

"Our baby."

"Yup."

He paused and looked at me. My tone of voice and facial expression told him that I was not playing.

He nodded his head up and down and said, "Alright Adara. I'll be here Sunday. I want to take you and Ava out this time. Is that cool?"

"Yes, that is."

"Aight. Good night."

Wes opened the door and walked out. I shut and locked the door. I put one of my hands on my head, and then I exhaled loudly. I felt tears begin to burn my eyes.

"No, Adara. You are not going to do this." I said out loud to myself.

I started shaking my hands rapidly to calm my nerves. I walked to the kitchen, poured a large glass of red wine, and took a few gulps. Wes had me in my feelings. He had me feeling ways that I didn't want to feel. I walked back to the living room and sat down on the couch with my glass of wine in hand. I took another gulp, and then I heard a knock at the door. I took another gulp, set the glass down, stood up, and walked to the door. I looked out the peep hole and saw Wes.

I opened the door and asked, "Did you forget something?"

"Yea."

"What? I can get it for you?"

Wes grabbed me and started kissing me. I tried to push him off, but quickly gave up the fight and let him kiss me. He pushed the door closed with his foot and pushed me up against the wall. I didn't stop him. I wanted it, but I didn't want to want it. As complicated as that sounds; that is how I felt. He started unbuttoning my jeans, and then I stopped him.

"Don't fight it Adara." he whispered.

"We can't do this."

"Yes, we can, and you want to as much as I do."

"I stood there silent for a few seconds. I was in my thoughts trying to figure out if I wanted to or not. He started kissing me again, and then he kissed my neck. Wes knew that is my spot. When I felt his soft lips touch my neck, tingles went through my body. I stopped him again.

"Adara. Let this happen. We both need it." he whispered.

I said, "Come on."

I locked the door and started walking to my bedroom. He removed his jacket and followed me. I started undressing in front of my bed, and he did the same. When I was finally fully nude, he paused and looked at me, and then he said, "Damn I missed you."

He kissed me again, laid me down, and kissed my body downwards. He kissed my lower lips and used his tongue to find my pearl. I closed my eyes as he licked it, kissed it, and sucked on it until I was singing slow tunes of passion to the ceiling. I opened my eyes to watch him and wound my hips a little to his groove. I knew I was making a mistake, but it was feeling too good to care. He looked up at me, stood up, and put his manhood inside of me. He put one of my legs on his shoulder and began putting his pound game on me. I wrapped my arms around him and tried to keep my moans low, so we wouldn't wake Ava.

"Tell me you miss me." he whispered.

"I miss you." I whispered back.

"I missed you too." he whispered.

Wes moaned a curse word, pulled out, pulled me to him by my leg, and flipped me over onto my stomach. He dove back inside of me. I almost yelled, so I covered my mouth with my hand. He grabbed a pillow and put it in front of me. I put my face in the pillow and cursed a few times. He grabbed my hair, and then he leaned down and whispered that he loved me in my ear. That made me lose it and my orgasm hit me hard. I let out a loud sound into the pillow and then I whispered, "Fuck, Wes."

"I told you that you needed this. I'm gonna give you another one."

He pulled out and laid on his back. "Come here." he demanded.

I climbed on top of him, put him inside of me, and started bouncing on him while he sucked on my nipples. He told me to kiss him again. I leaned down and began tongue kissing him as I bounced and wound my hips. He was right. He was going to make be bust them back to back. I felt it and bit my bottom lip. "Uh!" I grunted.

I paused, and he flipped me back over onto my back. He put my legs on his shoulder and continued to put it on me. He didn't stop until my legs were shaking.

"Shit baby, I'm about to cum." he moaned. He banged into me harder, and then he paused when he got his.

"Shit." he moaned, and then he laid down next to me in the bed.

"I'm going to go and check on Ava." I said. I stood up and tip toed to Ava's room. She was still sound asleep, so I quietly walked back to my room and climbed back in the bed next to Wes.

"Was, she still asleep?"

"Yes, thank God."

"I can leave ma." he said.

"You can stay." I said.

"Aight." he pulled me to him and kissed me.

***

The next morning, I was standing in the kitchen getting Ava's breakfast together. Wes walked out of my room fully dressed. He kissed my shoulder and said, "I'm gone."

"Um, about last night. That is all it was. last night. It can't happen again."

"Ok." Wes said. He kissed Ava on the top of her head and left.

Nia Rich

CHANEL

Chapter 18

I was sitting in an upscale bar listening to Lisa and the other wives laugh about an online video that went viral. Some chick bust her ass trying to be cute while twerking on a home installed stripper pole. The video had over a million views. It was funny, but I couldn't laugh because my mind was stuck on why my husband hadn't answered his phone all day. On top of that, he hadn't called, nor had he answered any of my text messages.

"Girl what's wrong? Are you still tripping about Orlando not calling yet?" Lisa asked.

"Girl don't trip. He is probably busy. He will call." Letisha said.

"It's just not like him to not call all day." I said.

"I used to be sitting by the phone waiting for Brandon to call all the time, but, now, I don't trip. If he calls, he calls. Kamira said.

"Me and Leonard went through that one time. Now, he knows better because I showed up on his ass." Letisha said.

Lisa laughed and said, "Girl you are crazy."

"I don't play." Letisha said.

Lisa said, "Me and Trav. have an understanding. He must call me at least before he goes to bed, so we can have some freaky deaky facetime sex.

"T.M.I." Tami said.

"What? Don't be acting like y'all don't do it too." Lisa said.

"Girl you know how Leonard and I get down." Letisha said.

Tami said, "Anyways. When he does call, just talk to him and let him know that you don't like it when he does that."

"Yea. You guys are still newlyweds. He is still learning you as you are him. Once Trav. and I had kids, a lot changed. He knows that he has to call home to check on the kids." Lisa said.

"Yea. I wouldn't worry about it. They'll be back tomorrow anyways." Kamira said.

"Anyways. Y'all know Donte's hoe ass is in the news again." Letisha said.

"Oh no. He can't keep his ass out of the news." Lisa said.

"Allegedly, he got another baby out there that he ain't claiming." Letisha said.

"Uh-uh girl." Kamira said.

"Yes, and guess who the baby's mama is?"

"Who?" Tami asked.

"That side chick hoe that be fucking all the players."

"That bitch with the pink hair?"

"It's blue now, but, yea, her."

"How the fuck did he end up knocking that nasty bitch up?" Kamira asked.

"I don't know girl. He should know better. Now, she's asking for child support." Letisha said.

"Ain't that like baby five for him?" Lisa asked.

"Yup." Letisha responded.

"He needs to slow down." Lisa said.

"Didn't your sister used to date him? She was at the wedding, right?" Lisa asked.

I said, "Yes."

"Shit, she dodged a bullet leaving his ass alone. There ain't enough money in the world to make me fuck with him." Letisha said.

"On another note, do you and Orlando plan to have any children?" Lisa asked.

"Eventually." I said.

"Have you met his other kids?" Letisha said.

"Yes, at the wedding." I responded.

"You better get on it quick while you're still young girl, so your body can snap back." Kamira said.

"Shit, Orlando got enough money to manufacture you a whole new body and face, if you wanted it. You've got all the time in the world girl." Letisha said.

All of us laughed. I was starting to like the wives. Letisha was a bit opinionated, but she was growing on me. They started talking about something else, and my mind went back to Orlando. I checked my phone again. No call.

Chapter 19

My phone ringing the next morning woke me up. Without pulling my blanket off my head, I reached over to the nightstand, grabbed it, and answered it while still under my blanket.

"Where have you been Orlando?" I asked.

My voice was low and groggy. He never called the night before. I hadn't talked to my husband in over twenty-four hours. That might not seem like a long time to some, but it was an extremely long amount of time for me. I was angry and hurt.

"Hey baby. I got your texts this morning. I'm sorry. I had a busy day yesterday."

"So busy that you couldn't call your wife?"

"I am sorry baby. By the time I made it back to my room, I just passed out."

"I would never go an entire day without calling you Orlando." I said. I pushed the cover off my head and sat up in the bed.

"I am sorry. I will make it up to you I promise."

"It's not about you making it up to me. It's about you not doing it again ever."

"Ok. I won't do it again baby. I promise. I love you."

"I love you too." I said irritably.

"I saw pictures of you and Lisa on your social media page."

"Yea we watched the game, and then went out for drinks. You did a good job babe."

"Thanks babe. You like them now, huh?

"They gossip a lot, but they're growing on me."

"That's good. I told you that you would like them. I'll be home later."

"Ok. I miss you."

"I've only been gone a day babe."

"One day without you is a lot."

He chuckled. "You miss this D. Don't worry I'm going to give it to you as soon as I get there."

"Whatever. I'll see you later."

***

Orlando walked in the house a few hours later carrying his travel bags. He dropped his stuff by the door and called out my name.

"I'm in the kitchen." I called out.

He walked into the kitchen and hugged me from behind. "Hey." Orlando said, and then he handed me a bag with a gift in it.

"What is this?" I asked.

"Open it."

I turned off the stove, took the bag from him, and opened it. There was a box inside with a pair of diamond earrings in it. I smiled, thanked him, and reached out to hug him.

"I thought that would put a smile on your face."

"It did babe. They are beautiful." I said.

He smiled and said, "I got something else that will make you smile."

"What?" I asked. He grabbed the crotch of his sweats. He picked me up and put me on the counter. He pulled my shorts off and put his stiff wood inside of me. I wrapped my legs around his waist and let him have me. He used the counter for leverage as he thrust into me. I tongue kissed him, and then I let him suck on my neck. I tilted my head back and enjoyed the feeling of my husband making love to me, but when I opened my eyes, I noticed a few scratch marks on his shoulder.

"Babe what are these scratches on your shoulder?" I asked as he continued to thrust into me.

"It's nothing. Me and the guys were goofing around in the locker room babe." Orlando replied.

He pounded into me some more, and then he pulled out and let himself go in his hand. I slid off the counter and he walked to the bathroom to wash his hands and clean up. I cleaned off the counter, and then I went into the bathroom to clean myself up. When we finished, we met back in the kitchen to eat. I made us plates of the food, and then we sat down at the island counter.

"I have to make a run after this." he said.

"Baby."

"What?"

"You just got home."

"So?"

"So? Don't you want to spend time with your wife?"

"Yes, baby I do, but I just got something to do with Trav. Tomorrow is my off day, so we will spend the entire day together."

"Ok." I said disappointedly.

He stood up and walked over to me. He wrapped his arm around my shoulder, and said, "Look, stop tripping. I love you."

"Yea, but it just seems like now that we are married, you don't have any time for us."

"Babe. Stop tripping."

"Ok." I sang.

The next day I was in the bathroom taking a shower livid. Not only did my husband walk in the house after three o'clock in the morning, but he got up the next morning and left without saying goodbye. I woke up in the bed alone. I called him, but he didn't answer, so I got out of bed and got into the shower. I was standing in the shower questioning my decision getting married to Orlando. I didn't anticipate things to be the way they were once we were married. My idea of what marriage was completely different than what it was turning out to be. We had been married for almost six months, and I had spent most of it alone. It wasn't like that when we were dating. Before the marriage, he couldn't get enough of me. He was constantly asking me to come over, spend the night, and flying me out to different states to see him during the season. Suddenly, being with me was no longer important.

I turned the shower off and stepped out to dry off. I needed to get dressed, so that I could do my video blog for my social media page. I had started my vlog page a month earlier and it was taking off pretty-well. I was doing fashion and make-up tutorials, and I was also doing product unboxing. The viewers were loving my channel, so my subscriptions, and view numbers were climbing. I oiled my body and put on a new Gucci dress and shoes that I bought. After I was finished getting ready, I walked to the room I had set up for my video blogs.

As I was finishing my blog, I heard my husband walk in the house downstairs, but it didn't sound like he was alone. I finished up the recording and walked down the stairs to see that my husband had his four kids with him. I instantly got irritated. I wasn't mad about the kids. I was angry because he didn't give me a heads up. I had plans to have a deep talk with him about how I was feeling about our marriage. I didn't know that he had plans to bring his children over.

"Hey babe!" he said when I reached the bottom of the stairs.

"Hi." I said, and then I gave him a hug.

"Y'all remember Ms. Chanel."

The two boys and two girls said, "Yes."

"Hi guys." I said cheerfully even though I was irritated.

Orlando said, "They're hungry babe. I was hoping that you could hook them up some lunch."

"Sure." I said. "What do you guys like? Sandwiches and chips?"

"Yea and pizza!" one of the younger boys said.

"Ok. I can do that. How about I make some sandwiches to tie you over until the pizza gets here? How does that sound?" I asked.

"Yaaay!" The younger girl said.

"Ok. Let's go to the kitchen." I said.

Orlando followed me and the kids to the kitchen. They sat around the kitchen island counter while I made sandwiches for them. Orlando ordered pizza from his phone. We sat and chatted with the kids until the pizza came. Orlando stood up to go pay for the pizza. After he put the pizza on the counter, he told me that he had to step out and he would be back.

"Where are you going Orlando?" I asked.

"I'll be back." he called back to me, and then he left out the door.

"Well, I guess it's just us." I said to the kids.

We ate pizza, played games, watched a movie, and then we settled on watching the Disney channel. Orlando still wasn't home. He had left me with his kids for hours. I looked out the window on my way to the kitchen to get the kids some more snacks. It was dark outside, and there was still no sign of Orlando. When I walked back to the living room, the older girl asked, "Where is daddy?"

"I don't know. I am going to go and call him." I said. I handed them some packages of fruit snacks, and then I headed to our office and called him.

"Where are you Orlando?" I asked when he answered.

"I am pulling up now." he said and hung up the phone.

I heard his truck pull into the driveway, so I met him at the door.

"Where have you been?" I whispered loudly. "The kids have been asking for you."

"I know. I'm sorry babe."

"Orlando. I don't want to hear that you are sorry anymore."

"Well, what do you want me to do? I got busy." he said, and then he brushed passed me and walked into the living room.

The younger girl jumped up and said, "Daddy!"

"Where were you?" The older girl asked.

"I had some things to do. Let's go." he said. All the kids stood up and followed him out the door. He didn't even say goodbye to me. He just walked out, waited for the kids to get into his vehicle, and then he drove off.

Chapter 20

After Orlando walked out of the door, I cleaned the mess that his kids left behind. I pulled a bottle of red wine out of our wine bottle holder, grabbed a glass from the cabinet, and walked into the living room. I sat down on the couch and found one of my favorite reality shows to watch on our huge, flat screen television.

When I looked up, a couple of hours had gone by, the bottle of wine was gone, and Orlando was just walking back in the door. I was fuming, tipsy, and done with the bullshit. I walked to the door to meet him.

"Where have you been? It doesn't take two hours to drop your kids off." I said as I stormed towards him.

"What are you talking about?"

"I'm talking about you constantly being out late when you have a wife at home, and then you leave me here with your kids! Kids that you never told me were coming!"

"Aye, I don't want to hear this Chanel."

"So, I am just supposed to be ok with you leaving me in this house with your kids all day!?"

"You're their step mom. You shouldn't have a problem with that."

"I wouldn't have had a problem with it had I known beforehand! You just pop up with them as if you didn't tell me yesterday, that we were going to spend your day off together!"

"Look, I don't have time for this shit. You're bugging out Chanel."

"Oh, I'm bugging out!? You keep coming in this house at all times of the night like you're not married!" I yelled.

Orlando charged at me with his finger pointed in my face and yelled, "Look, I said I don't have time for this shit, so shut the fuck up talking to me!" He backed me up against the wall in the hallway.

"I don't want to hear shit else!" he yelled again, and then he stormed off.

My eyes welled up with tears. I turned, walked up to our master bedroom, walked into the bathroom, and shut the door. I sat on the edge of the tub and started crying. I don't think that I have ever cried that hard in my life. I cried for a while, and then Orlando came to the bathroom door. He started talking me through the door.

"Baby I'm sorry for yelling."

"I don't want to hear it Orlando." I said through tears.

"Open the door baby please." he said.

I wiped my eyes with the back of my hand and opened the door. He came towards me with his arms outstretched. I let him hug me.

"I didn't mean to make you cry. You were just coming at me so harsh. I guess I just reacted. I promise I am going to do better ok?"

I nodded my head up and down.

Nia Rich

"Come on let's go to bed."

ADARA

Chapter 22

I was lying in bed looking at the ceiling again with Wes lying next to me. That situation that happened that wasn't supposed to happen again; happened again, and again, and again. It had happened so many times that I'd lost count. It was happening every Sunday for three months. Wes had become my Sunday night creep. He was giving me the good D that I wanted, and he was giving me the cuddle action that I needed every now and then, but I still didn't want to be with him.

"We should stop playing and go ahead and make this official again." he said.

"I don't think so Wes." I said.

"Why not?"

"Because I don't want to do that. I mean, what we are doing is cool, but I don't want more than that."

"Why Adara? I've changed."

"I don't know that."

"You see me."

"Only one a week."

"That's your choice."

"For a reason."

"Come on babe. We love each other, and we should do this for our daughter."

"Our daughter is fine. I'm sorry Wes, but I don't trust you. I know that you are messing with some chicks; especially that chick that I got into a fight with."

"No. I'm not fucking with her. Listen, I love you. I need you. I don't want to be here just one day a week. I want to be here all the time and be a family like we were supposed to be."

"No."

"No, what? You don't want that?"

"No, I don't Wes."

"Why do you have to be such a hard ass all the time?"

"When I was soft, you ran over me. I can't let you hurt me like that again."

"I'm not going to hurt you. I love you Adara. I only love you. I know you love me too."

"I always will."

"Well let's work past this together."

"There's nothing to work past."

"Aight. I'm going to leave it alone. Come here and let me hold you. I don't care what you say; you know that you miss me holding you every night, and you know this is still my pussy.

"Shut up." I said, and then I laughed.

I let him pull me closer to him, and we cuddled for the rest of the night.

***

I was sitting on my couch watching Ava play with her toys on the floor. My phone started ringing. I knew that it was Miles calling from a video chat app because the ringtone was different than my normal phone ringtone. I picked up my phone and swiped the green phone icon to the right to answer it. I angled the phone, so he could see a clear image of me.

"Hi!" I said into the camera when Mile's face appeared.

"Hey beautiful. How are things going? he asked.

"They have been going well. Ava wasn't feeling good, so she kept me up the last few nights."

"Oh no. What was wrong with her."

"She had a cold."

"How does she feel now?"

"Oh, she is better now, but I am feeling sick"

"That's not good. You gotta stay well, so I can see your pretty face every day." he said.

I smiled into the camera, and he did the same.

"I said, "Thank you, Miles."

"You're welcome, so I was thinking. We haven't seen each other since the wedding, and I would love to see you. We've been doing this phone thing for half a year."

"I know. I was thinking the same thing. I want to see you too."

"Well, I was thinking that you could come down here for a weekend. We can spend some time with each other. If you want to bring Ava you can, or if you would like for me to make babysitting arrangements for my daughter, I can do that too."

"Maybe we should just hang out first before introducing each other to our children."

'I think that is a great idea. You should let me know when you are free, so I can book your ticket."

"Oh no. I can buy my own ticket Miles."

"I want to buy your ticket."

"No, I can't let you do that."

"Adara. It's ok. I know that you're an independent woman but let me do something nice for you."

I smiled, and then I said, "Alright."

He smiled and said, "I got to get my daughter in bed. Talk to you tomorrow? Same time?"

"Yes."

"Ok goodnight. Sweet dreams."

I disconnected the video chat and smiled again as I set my phone back on the coffee table.

"Come on big girl. Time for bed."

I stood up, picked her up, and walked with her to her bedroom.

***

"I had a blast with the baller dude in Chicago girl." Nikita said.

"Oh, your sidepiece?"

"Yes girl. I stayed the weekend with him, and all we did was fuck, drink, and sleep."

"Did y'all go anywhere?"

"Yea. We went out to a club, got drunk, went back to the hotel room, fucked, and then we went to sleep."

I laughed. "Sounds like a blast."

"I had too much fun girl. That dude's D is amazing and his head game; Oooo wee."

"Ok cousin." I slapped hands with her.

"What's up with the doctor?"

"He wants to get together."

"It's about time."

"I know."

"You're really feeling the doctor, huh?"

"I like him a lot. He's different than other guys that I've dated. He is sweet, attentive, consistent. He isn't trying to move extra fast like Donte, or come with that, 'what's up shorty' game like Wes. He makes me smile.

"Aww look at how your face lights up when you talk about him."

"Ok. You're doing too much right now. I am done with this subject." I said. Nikita laughed.

"Shit girl. Look at the time. I am running late picking up my son. Are we still hanging this weekend?"

"Yup. Kyra invited us over for dinner. Seven sharp."

"Alright. I'll see you there."

"Nikita rushed out of the shop. I looked down at my phone and smiled when I saw a text message from Miles.

I can't wait to see you.

I sent a reply text, and then I finished sweeping up my shop floor.

Chapter 23

It was a Friday, Wes was at my house, and we were back at it again. My mom had Ava for the weekend, and I don't know how I let Wes talk me into letting him come by, but he was there putting it down like he always did. That time we were really going at it because Ava wasn't there, and we didn't have to be quiet. I asked myself why I was doing it, and then Wes hit my spot and put all my focus on him. I started moaning loudly.

"That's it, right there, ain't it?" he asked.

"Yes, stay right there. Don't stop." I moaned.

"Fuck." he grunted.

When he said that, my splash waterfalls were uncontrollable. I whined loudly as my body jerked and shivered.

"Oh my, God." I cried out as he let himself go, and then he sat up and chuckled.

"Look at you. You be loving this shit." he said.

I laughed and said, "Whatever Wes. You're full of yourself."

"I be putting that shit down and you know it." he said as he laid next to me.

"Maybe." I said.

He laughed. "You gonna give me my props. I just had you like an ocean. My pound game is serious."

I said, "Aight you put it down."

"That's right. I always do. Now, come here." I rolled over into his arms.

He kissed me and said, "You know you mine, right?"

"Wes don't start. We just had a good session."

"And we're going to have another one, but the fact still remains. You're my woman, and you always will be. I don't care what you're talking about. This is mine. You are mine. Period."

"Whatever Wes. We're not together."

"You love me, don't you?"

I smacked my lips and looked up at the ceiling.

He chuckled, "I don't know why you be trying to act hard, when you know that you love me."

"Loving you doesn't change how I feel about our situation."

"Like I said, You mine. This mine. That's that."

***

Wes took me out to breakfast the next day. We went to an International House of Pancakes, and then he talked me into going to the mall across the street to shop for Ava. Somehow, we ended up at an afternoon movie, and then we went out to lunch. I was having fun with Wes, and I wasn't even trying to. After lunch we ended up back at my house, in my bed, giving each other the business until it was time for me to go and hang out with my girls as Kyra's house. He had me hollering, cursing, and saying things that I didn't want to say.

"Tell me you love me." he said between thrusts.

"I love you."

"This is mine?"

"Yes."

"I love you too bae, and we are going to be together. You hear me?"

"Yes, I hear you Wes."

I busted, he busted, and then I got up to shower and get dressed.

Chapter 24

Kyra's house is what I call earthy. The color scheme of her house is earth tones. There is a mixture of browns, tans and maroons with a splash of burnt orange and mustard yellow here and there. She has numerous potted plants throughout the house, and she is always burning incense and candles. Her home felt warm and inviting. I looked around at the various pictures of Nubian Queens and Goddesses on her walls as we walked through her house to the living room.

"I am so glad that you ladies could come." Kyra said to me and Nikita.

"Thanks for inviting us. Your home is beautiful. I said.

"Thank you." she said. "Bianca, my sister, and my best friend should be here soon."

"Girl where did you get this art?" I asked.

"Various places. Mostly online."

"I love it." I said. I looked at the vase of sunflowers on her coffee table, and then my ears picked up the sound of jazz music coming through the speakers. The ambience was so peaceful.

"Make yourself comfortable. Would you ladies like a glass of wine?"

"Yes." I said.

"Girl you know that I will take one." Nikita said.

Kyra giggled and walked away. I've always admired how soft and feminine Kyra is. Everything she does is like silk; almost effortless. She speaks softly. She never moves quickly, never raises her voice, never sweats, and never looks stressed. She never looks like she has a bad day. She carries herself like Queen always. Made me wonder what her boyfriend was like.

Kyra returned to the living room with two empty glasses and a bottle of wine. She handed me and Nikita the glasses, and then poured wine from the bottle into them. She refilled a glass of wine that she already had on the table.

"So, what is new? I only get to hear bits and pieces at the salon."

Nikita couldn't wait to tell her business. "Girl you know that I am still talking to that ball player that I met in New York." she said.

"Oh yea? How is that going?" Kyra asked.

"He said that he is going to fly me down there again. Next weekend." Nikita said.

"So, you're living the good life, huh?" Kyra asked.

"She is living a double life." I said.

Kyra giggled. "I assume that your baby dad doesn't know yet."

"Oh, hell no, and he will never know. You know women are better at cheating than men are. I got this on lock." Nikita said.

Kyra laughed, and then she asked me, "What about you?"

"I am going to Atlanta to visit the doctor soon."

"Good for you girl. It's about time."

"That is what I said." Nikita said.

"Where is your boyfriend?" Nikita asked Kyra.

"He is still out of town, but he will be back tomorrow."

"I know that you can't wait to see him."

"Something like that." Kyra said, and then the doorbell caught her attention. "That should be the rest of the ladies." she said and stood up to walk to the door.

She opened the door and said, "Hi!" she reached out to hug each person, and then she moved out the way, so they could walk in.

"Hey Chica's!" Bianca said when she saw us. She walked over to hug us before sitting down on the couch next to me. Kyra introduced the other ladies.

"This is my sister April and my best friend Destiny."

I was instantly annoyed when I saw Destiny. I remembered her. She was with Lesley the night that I got into the fight. I was ready to put my glass of wine down, walk out, and fire Kyra.

"Wait a minute. Aren't you Illi-J's daughter?" Nikita said to Destiny.

She giggled and answered, "Yes. Aw great now you guys are going to think I am some spoiled rich kid."

"No, we're not girl. Nice to meet you. I thought your family lived in Atlanta."

We do. I am up here visiting my grandma and this chick." Destiny said.

"How did you two, meet?" Nikita asked.

"At the Bonners Brothers hair show. We've been tight ever since." Destiny said.

"That's cool girl, well nice to meet you." Nikita said.

"Well, anyways. Since you are all here. I wanted to tell you that I had this gathering to celebrate us as women. The beautiful, hard-working, independent women that we are. I am also celebrating my two-year anniversary of being cancer free. I wanted to share this moment with my beautiful and strong queens."

All of us said congrats, but her confession shocked me. I never knew that she had battled cancer. It made me think about how short life was, and then I thought about Miles. I started to feel like life was too short to be taking my time on something that felt right. Kyra told us to follow her to the table, so we could eat, and then Destiny asked if she could speak to me for a second.

We walked to a sun porch area of the house and faced each other.

"First I want to say nice to formerly meet you. You know Lesley, right?"

"I wouldn't say that I know her." I said with an attitude.

"I don't want any beef. I know that you don't know me, but I didn't want it to be awkward. I know that you probably remember me from the night you two got into that fight. I just want to disassociate myself from that situation. Lesley is my cousin, and I was in town that night. We were just supposed to be going out. I knew she had a guy she was dealing with, but I didn't know anything about that situation. I was completely shocked about the fight, and then I was pissed at her. I don't know what kind of relationship you had with him, but I don't agree with women fighting over men at all, you know. I have always felt like and still feel like she can do better, but she chooses to continue to mess with him.

"Wait. what?"

"You didn't know she was still dealing with him?"

"No."

"Yea, she is pregnant, right now."

"How far along?"

"Like four or five months.

I shook my head.

"Is he your boyfriend?"

"He is my baby's father."

"Oh. No disrespect, but I can't stand him."

"Trust me the feeling is mutual."

She giggled, and then I said, "Um, well thank you for being honest. I can't lie; I was a little angry when I first saw you, but I understand. I appreciate you being a woman about it."

"Thank you."

We hugged and walked back to the table with the other ladies. Part of me didn't care because it was expected and me and Wes were not together, and the other part of me was irritated because I was sure that he knew, and never said anything to me about it. *Typical Wes.* I thought. He always had a secret hiding in the bushes. I thought about when I found out about his wife and kids, and when I found out about his baby mama Raven, and then when I found out about him and Lesley while I was pregnant with Ava. There was always something with him, and that was the reason that I was done with him. I didn't know how I had let myself slip. I was irritated, but I decided that I wasn't going to say anything to Wes. I wanted to see how long it was going to take him to tell me.

Chapter 25

I was standing in the kitchen cooking lunch for Ava. Wes was in the living room watching Ava play with her toys and watch children's learning shows. All was peaceful and then suddenly Wes stormed into the kitchen with my phone in hand.

"Who the fuck is the dude Miles calling you?"

I quickly turned to face Wes. "First of all, give me my phone. Second, that is none of your business."

"The fuck it ain't my business. You got some dude around my daughter!?" Wes asked angrily.

"You don't know what you are talking about and you need to give me my phone." I said as I walked towards him with my hand outstretched.

"No. I'm not giving you shit until you tell me who the fuck Miles is."

"You need to calm down. Like I said, that is not your business. I can talk to whoever I want Wes. We are not together."

"We not together huh? So, what was all that shit you were talking the other day? You love me. It's mine, and all that shit?"

"We were having sex Wes."

"So, you just say anything during sex?"

"Whatever. Give me my phone. I am not having this conversation."

"We are having this conversation! You couldn't tell me that you were fucking some other dude and bringing him around my daughter?!"

"Wes, I don't owe you an explanation, but if you must know, Miles is a friend of mine, we have never had sex, and he has never seen Ava, and since you all up in arms about what I have going on, let's talk about what you have going on because I wasn't even going to say anything. You got your nerve to be standing here fussing at me about who I'm not fucking, when you know damn well your still fucking Lesley, and she is pregnant right now."

I didn't want to bring it up, but I had to pull my trump card. Wes gave me the craziest look; like he was shocked at what I said about Lesley.

"I don't even know what you're talking about." he said.

"Oh really?" I asked sarcastically. "So, should I call her cousin right now, and have her tell you. Will that make it clear enough?"

"You on that bullshit." he said.

"No, you are. You lied. You told me that you weren't messing with her anymore, but in the back of my mind I knew that you were. That is why I couldn't even take anything that you said seriously. What is this? Baby number five and baby momma number four? You can't even keep it one hundred with your shit. That's why I've been done, and I should have stayed being done with your ass, so give me my damn phone, and get out of my house. We're not doing this no more. You can call when you want to see Ava, and I will bring her to you."

He gave me an angry stare for a second, and then he said, "Man whatever." he handed my phone to me and walked out. He slammed the door closed.

Nia Rich

Chanel

Chapter 26

Orlando turned his phone off. I called again just to make sure. The call went straight to voicemail. I exhaled loudly, and then slammed my phone down on my bed. I was so frustrated that I felt like I wanted to scream. I looked at the time. It was after midnight and I had called Orlando at least ten time before he turned his phone off, and ten times after he turned it off. I left several messages, and text messages, and he didn't respond, nor did he call back.

I slid out of bed and walked bare foot through our bedroom, down the stairs, and into the kitchen. I pulled a bottle of wine out of the cabinet and poured a large glass. I needed something to calm my nerves. I called my best friend Melanie. I needed someone to talk me through my feelings. Her phone went to voicemail.

"Ugggh." I grunted.

She never answered when she was with her boyfriend. I decided to try Lisa. I knew that it was late, but both of our husbands played for the same team and they were out of town at an away game. I put my hand to my face as I listened to her phone ringing on speaker phone. She picked up on the third ring.

"Hello?" she answered. Her voice was groggy, so I knew that she was probably sleep.

"Hey girl, I am sorry to wake you."

"It's ok. What's wrong?"

"I am so frustrated right now. Orlando turned his phone off, after he isn't answering it. I'm just so over it." I started tearing up. "I think I made a mistake marrying him."

I knew for sure that I had made a mistake and I couldn't call the one person that loves me the most because I was too embarrassed to admit it to Adara. I talked so much shit about her baby daddy dogging her out and here is my rich man doing the same fuck boy shit to me. I looked at the huge diamond on my finger and took another sip of wine.

"Girl, you are just going through it right now, but it is going to be ok."

"Thank you. I am sorry that I woke you up."

"It's ok girl. Let's get together tomorrow. Come over in the morning. We'll have breakfast, mimosa's, and some girl chat. How does that sound?"

"That sounds good. Thank you, Lisa."

"It's no problem at all. I understand. Trust me."

I hung up and walked with my glass of wine back up to my bedroom.

***

Lisa was kind enough to cook breakfast and keep me company while I was going through the motions about Orlando. I was sick and tired of his bullshit. I had quit my job and totally became a housewife at his request and he was treating me like crap.

"Thanks for all of this." I said to Lisa before taking a sip of the mimosa she made for me.

"It's no problem at all. I told you I went through the same thing with my husband years ago."

"You stuck it out and you two seem happy."

"Yea we are now, but we went through a lot to get to this point."

"So, do you think that I should stick it out?"

"I mean, my husband finally got it together. It took for me to threaten a divorce for him to make those changes though. I say, you got to do what's best for you and your situation. If you think you can stick it out, go ahead."

"I don't know. Right now, I am ready to give this ring back and be done with this shit."

"I am sorry that you are going through this."

"Thank Lisa."

"If you ever need me girl, for anything, just call me."

"Ok." I said, and then I took a sip of my mimosa.

"So, what's up with your girl that you brought to the game a few weeks ago?"

"Who Melanie? That is my best friend."

"Hmm. Is she a jersey chaser?"

"What is a jersey chaser?"

"A chick who only goes after professional sports players."

"No, but she is dating a ball player."

"Who? I've never seen her. Does he play on the same team as our husbands?"

"Yup, but I've been sworn to secrecy."

"Oh ok."

"It's still kind of new, and he doesn't want a bunch of people in his business, so she doesn't come to games much."

Lisa took a sip of her mimosa and said, "I'm going to be honest with you. I wasn't feeling her."

I chuckled. "Why?"

"I don't know. She was just a little too friendly with the guys in my opinion."

"That's just her. She is just a friendly person."

"Honestly, she seemed like a groupie disguised as a best friend. I'm just saying, be careful with that because bitches like that ain't shit."

I laughed. "Wow. Ok." I said.

Melanie had never rubbed me the wrong way. I took it as Lisa hating because she doesn't like any good-looking woman coming around and enticing her man. I brushed what she said off my shoulder, and then my phone rang.

"It's Orlando." I said.

"They must be back in town which means my husband will be home soon."

"What's up." Orlando said when I answered. He didn't sound like he was in a good mood.

"You tell me. I've been calling you all night." I said irritably.

"My phone died. Where are you?"

"I'm at Lisa's."

"Come home now." he said angrily.

My face frowned, and then I said, "Alright." I hung up and looked at Lisa. "He wants me to come home.

F—k Boy 2

"Alright girl. Well, you know that you can hit me up anytime. I hope that everything works out for you two."

"Thanks again for all of this. I needed it."

"Anytime girl.

199 | P a g e

Chapter 27

I pulled my car into the garage thirty minutes later. I touched the hood of Orlando's car to see if he had driven it at all. It was cold to the touch which meant he had not left out of the house yet since he'd been home. Orlando came storming around the corner when I walked into the house.

"Where the fuck have you been?" he asked angrily.

"I already told you. I was at Lisa's house."

"For what?"

"Because I was stressed, and I needed to get out of this house. Are you just going to act like you didn't ignore my phone calls, and then turn your phone off last night?"

"I want you home, when I come home." Orlando said angrily.

I grimaced, and then I said, "You didn't answer your phone all night Orlando. You turned it off, and I know that you saw me calling you."

"I told you. My phone died."

"You couldn't put it on a charger and call me back?"

"I passed out. I wasn't thinking about no charger, and like I said; I want you home when I get home. I don't want you out in the streets yacking and cackling with Lisa and those gossiping ass bitches."

"You were the one who introduced to them and told me to hang with them."

"What the fuck did I say?"

"Excuse me? You still haven't given me an honest reason why you ignored me all night Orlando! You come home giving orders like your King Tut."

He glared at me, started yelling, and pointing his finger at me. "I already told you what happened! I'm not going to keep going back and forth with you about some bullshit! I want you home period.

"I'm not going to keep going through this bullshit with you! Either you get it together or we are getting a divorce!" I yelled back.

He grabbed my face, pushed me up against a wall, and yelled, "Who the fuck is you talking to? Don't you ever say that shit to me again!? Now leave me the fuck alone!"

Orlando marched out of the garage door, slammed it, got into his car, and left.

I stood frozen. I was in shock. I didn't know if I want to cry or run, so I just stood there in silence for a few minutes trying to process what had just happen.

***

I woke up the next morning to Orlando kissing me on the cheek. I moved, but I didn't open my eyes. I didn't feel like being bothered with him after what happened the day before. Orlando stayed out the entire day after he left. He didn't return home until late that night, and I didn't bother to call him, nor did I talk to him when he made it home. I was up when he got into the bed with me, but I played like I was sleep. I laid there in my thoughts until I finally fell asleep.

"I'm sorry baby." he whispered in my ear. He shook me a little, so I opened my eyes. I saw his bald head and puppy dog eyes.

"Baby I love you. I'm sorry." he repeated, but I didn't respond. Orlando kissed my lips, and then he bent down and put his head under the blanket.

"Orlando stop." I said. He ignored me and pushed my night gown up. He started kissing my peach while my panties were still on, and then he pulled my panties off. He put his face in my middle and tongue kissed my pearl until I wasn't mad anymore. He had me singing orgasmic tunes to the ceiling. I closed my eyes when I reached my peak, and when I opened them, Orlando was on top of me putting his hard manhood into me. First, he spread my legs open, and then he put them on his shoulders. That was his favorite position. He thrusted, pounded, grinded, long stroked it, short stroked it, and then he flipped me over and did it all again from the back. He whispered that he loved me when he busted, and then he laid next to me.

"I know that I've been messing up and I am sorry. I shouldn't have yelled at you. I was mad that we lost the game and I was stressed. I love and appreciate you and I want to show you. We are going to spend the day together. No kids; just us. I am going to take you shopping. Hit up your favorite stores and do whatever you want. Would you like that?"

"Yes."

"Do you love me?"

"Yes."

"Do you forgive me?"

"Yes."

"Are you sure?"

I smiled and said, "Yes."

"Aight. Let's take a shower and get dressed."

ADARA

Chapter 28

Nikita stopped by my house after work to chat and get caught up. We hadn't seen each other in a couple of weeks. I was booked up at the salon, and she had been busy with work. She had just got back from a weekend with her sidepiece and I know she wanted to fill me in on the details. She took off her coat, hung it in the closet by my door, and then she took off her Ugg boots and put them on the floor mat.

"It's cold out there." she said.

"I know. I haven't been back out there since I got home from the shop."

"When was the last time you talked to Chanel?"

"It has been a while. I tried to call her, but she didn't answer."

"Well, anyways, girl when can you do this hair because I sweat it out over this weekend girl."

"You and the baller again?"

"Girl yes, that man was putting it down something serious."

I laughed and asked, "Did you have to put ice on the cookie again."

"Yea, but girl. I ain't even going to tell you the things I did with ice to him."

"Oooo you're nasty."

"Oh, and grapefruit."

"Oh, you went there too?" I laughed and slapped hands with her.

"Look what he gave me." she said, and then she held out her arm.

"This is nice. Are they real diamonds?"

"That is what he says."

"Well you sure deserve it. All those stunts you were doing."

She laughed and said, "Um hum, so girl. What's been up with you? Did you book the tickets to go and see the doctor?"

I scratched my head and said, "Well, girl I'm pregnant."

"Wait. WHAT!? How? The doctor came up here and you didn't tell me."

"I'm pregnant by Wes."

Nikita started laughing. "Hold up. Hold the fuck up. Wes!?"

"Stop laughing cousin. It's not funny."

"I thought you weren't fucking? When did Wes come back into the picture?"

"Long story short, we were messing around for a few months."

"A few months!"

"It wasn't deep. It was just sex."

"You were creeping around with your baby daddy and you didn't say shit bitch! I am mad at you! I told you that you wanted him to tap that again!" Nikita chuckled.

I hit her in the arm and said, "Shut up."

"No, I'm not going to shut up. You, sneaky bitch!"

"I'm serious cousin. I am messed up over this. I don't know what to do. I do not want to have another baby; especially not by Wes, and how am I going to tell Miles? He was under the impression that I was not having sex. I really like him, but he is not going take me seriously carrying another man's child."

"Girl, I don't even know what to tell you on this situation."

"I've been thinking about having an abortion, but it makes me feel like I am killing my child; a child that deserves to live. Then, I feel like, why bring another child into this dysfunctional situation?"

"Do you want to be with Wes?"

"I mean, I love Wes, but he cannot be the man that I need him to be and that is the reason that I don't want to be with him. You know I just found out that he has another baby on the way with Lesley that he ain't claiming."

"I know, and that is some trifling shit right there."

I exhaled and said, "I don't know what I am going to do cousin."

"Does Wes know?"

"Not yet. We haven't really been talking much lately unless it's about Ava."

"You could have an abortion."

"Yea I could. I mean this is going to be baby number six for Wes, and I am pretty much going to be doing everything by myself, but this time with two kids." I shook my head. "I fucked up cousin." I said as I I rubbed my forehead.

"Awwww." she said. She scooted next to me and hugged me. "Everything is going to be ok. I support whatever you choose to do.

"Thank you. Miles is going to be done with me."

***

I didn't know how I was going to tell Miles about the situation I was in. Everything was going so good with us. I felt like I didn't have to tell him anything because we weren't together, but I didn't want to be like Wes and keep need to know information a secret. I felt like Miles was such a good guy that he deserved to know the truth. That I had slipped up with my baby daddy.

I was sitting at that shop in deep thought. I was the only one there. It was morning and the other stylists hadn't made it in yet. I had gotten there early to open for a client, but they canceled at the last minute. I wasn't tripping because I was feeling a little tired. That pregnancy was different than when I was pregnant with Ava. I wasn't extremely sick like I was when I was pregnant with her. I was just feeling more exhausted than usual. I wouldn't have known that I was pregnant, if I didn't keep up with my monthly cycle like I do. I knew right away that I was pregnant.

I heard the door open and the sound of wet shoes on the tile floor. I stood up and walked from the backroom to the front of the salon to see who it was. I knew that it was one of my stylists.

Kyra said, "Good morning."

"Good morning doll. How are you?" I walked over to her and gave her a hug.

"I am fabulous. How are you Queen?"

"I don't know. I am this; that this morning." I said.

"Oh no. What's wrong?" she asked as she started to set up her station.

"I just have a lot on my mind." I said.

"Yea?" she asked, and then she looked at me. "Do you want to talk about it?"

I didn't know Kyra that well, but her energy made me feel like I could talk to her. I was never the type to tell everyone my business like my cousin Nikita, but I needed some perspective from another person that wasn't family.

"Do you mind lending me your ear for a little bit?"

"I don't mind at all." Kyra said. She sat down in her stylist chair and gave me her undivided attention.

"I just don't know what I want to do. I am pregnant again."

"By your baby's father?" she asked.

"Yes." I said.

"Oh wow."

"I know, and I am trying to figure out if I want to keep it because you know that we aren't together, and I have started to like someone else."

"Which is the doctor."

"Yes."

"Ok. Would you like my opinion?"

"Yes, I would."

"Well, obviously there are still some feelings there or you wouldn't have messed with him at all. Maybe it's worth giving another try. Some things do deserve a second chance. I mean I know how much you loved him from what you told me, but if you feel in your heart that it's not worth a second chance than you have to do what's right for you."

"What about the doctor?"

"If it was meant to be with the doctor, it will be, and when the dust settles, he will be there as a friend, but if it wasn't meant for y'all than you two will go on with your lives. I am a firm believer that everything happens for a reason. Like how I am the first one in this shop today." She smiled.

I smiled. "I was thinking about getting an abortion."

"Personally, I believe that every child deserves a chance, but I understand that certain circumstances lead to making that kind of decision, so you have to do what is best for you, but keep *you* at the forefront of your decision because at the end of the day, it's going to be *you* that will be responsible for taking care of the child."

I smiled at her. "Thank you, Kyra. I appreciate it."

"No problem. Come here mama. Let me give you a hug." she said.

I walked over to her and hugged her.

"Now I have a question for you." I said after we embraced.

"Ok."

"Why didn't you tell me that you were a cancer survivor?"

"It's not something that I like to talk about. It was a tough time in my life, and I didn't know if I was going to live. I choose to share it with people I feel close to, and I consider you ladies to be like my family now."

"What kind of cancer was it?

"Breast."

"Wow. That's crazy."

"Yea it was a lot to deal with."

"Thank you for sharing. It really touched me."

"You're welcome."

"How does your man feel about it?"

"Oh, he was there through it all. We've been together for a long time."

"How long?"

"Ten years. Since I was twenty-one."

"No marriage?"

"No. Not yet at least."

"Wow. We have to get you two married."

She chuckled and said, "Well, I mean, it feels like we already are. He is my best friend, but you know, all relationships have their problems, so we'll see."

"Do you have plans for Christmas Eve?" she asked.

"No. I usually go over to my mom's house Christmas day."

"Awesome. Christmas Eve I usually cook and host a gathering at my house. I invite my loved ones and their families over, so I would love for everyone from this shop to come. Bring the kids. I will have treats and toys for them, and my man will be there, so you will get a chance to meet him."

"Ok, well Ava and I will be there."

"Should I be expecting Wes too?"

I laughed, "Maybe."

"Ok." she smiled, and then the sound of the doorbell caught our attention. It was her client showing up for their hair appointment.

Kyra stood up, and then she said, "Hello. Come on in."

I stood up and walked back to my office.

Chapter 29

Wes called and asked if we could talk. I told him that he could stop by because I wanted to hear what he had to say and talk with him about our current situation that he knew nothing about. He told me that he would be over in an hour, so I felt like it would be the best time to talk to my friend Miles. I tapped the screen on my cell phone to call him. The phone rang a couple of times, and then he answered.

"Hello beautiful."

"Hey Miles. How are you?"

"I am doing well. How about you?"

"I am doing fine. I am happy that the holiday season is here."

"Yea me too. What's wrong? You don't seem like yourself."

I don't know where the tears came from. They just started flowing.

"What's wrong baby? Why are you crying?"

"I just feel so horrible. I don't know how to tell you this because I like you so much."

"I like you too, but what's wrong?"

I exhaled, wiped a few tears, and then I said, "I'm pregnant."

"Oh wow." Miles said disappointedly. He sounded like I had just let the air out of his balloon.

"I know Miles. I mean, I was so excited to come down there and see you, and I just fucked up. I'm so sorry because I feel like I misled you."

"I mean, I can't say that I'm not hurt." he said.

"I know." I barely got the words out because my tears started falling again.

"Listen, don't cry. I can get over it Adara. Is the baby by your child's father?"

"Yes."

"I mean it was to be expected. We haven't seen each other since the wedding. I would have been a fool to believe that you weren't seeing other people. I was seeing other people. I just had high hopes for us, but it's ok. Life happens. It's nothing to beat yourself up over. I still like you, and we're friends. We've been friends, and we're going to continue to be friends."

"Thank you, Miles."

"You and your child's father should try to work it out. You child deserves to have both parents, if it is possible, and now there is a new baby coming, so it's worth a try. I am here for you, if you need me for whatever. You hear me? Anything. Just call me."

I wiped my tears. "Ok. Thank you. You're such a good person."

"You are too Adara."

I smiled and said, "Um, I have to go."

"Alright well just hit me up whenever babe."

I hung up with Miles just as I heard Wes close his car door. I looked at Ava and said, "Daddy's here."

Her face lit up and she ran to the door. I followed her and opened the door before he made it to the steps. Ava started jumping around with excitement. She was so happy to see her dad. I wish I felt the same, but I was not happy to see him, nor was I happy about our situation.

"Hey baby!" he said.

He reached down to picked her up. He kissed her on the cheek and she laughed. I closed the door and walked back into the living room to sit down. He put her down, so he could take his coat and boots off, and then he picked her back up and walked to the living room with her in his arms.

"What's wrong with you? Why do you look like you've been crying?" he asked.

"I'm just stressed." I said.

"About what?" he asked.

I bypassed the question. "You said that you wanted to come over here and talk about something, so what's up?" I asked.

He put Ava down on the floor. She walked over to her toys.

"Look I came over here because I wanted to talk to you about Lesley."

"You're ready to tell the truth?"

"Yes, I am."

"Ok, I am ready to hear it."

"Yes. I was still fucking with Lesley during the time we were not together."

I rolled my eyes and crossed my arms, and then he said, "I know that makes you mad, but we weren't together, and you weren't talking to me."

"So, you go and fuck with the bitch that I got into a fight?"

"Adara, it wasn't right away. At the time, it had been months since me and you had talked. She came over to cuz's house and shit happened."

"So, you were fucking me and her at the same time?"

"No. By the time me and you started messing around, her and I weren't talking at all."

"You knew about the baby?"

"Yes, I did, but me and you had started messing around and I didn't want to kill the vibe."

"So, you lied."

"No, no I didn't. I wasn't messing with Lesley. I didn't tell you because I want to be with you and I didn't want to do anything that would mess up that chance."

"Why do I always have to get your business from a third party?" I asked angrily.

"I was going to tell you eventually."

"When? When the baby is here?"

"Possibly." he said.

I shook my head.

"Well I'm just keeping it real." he said.

"Should have kept it real from the gate."

"Adara."

"Alright. I guess, thank you for telling me after the fact." I said with an attitude.

"Are you happy now?" he asked.

"Sure." I said.

"Good." Wes said, and then he looked at Ava.

"Well, I guess it's a good time to tell you that I am pregnant."

He looked back at me and asked, "What?"

"I'm pregnant Wes."

"Are you serious?" he asked.

"No. I'm lying." I said sarcastically. "Yes, I am serious." I said.

Wes smiled, put his hand to his mouth, and stood up. He walked over and sat down next to me. Wes put his hand on my stomach and smiled again.

"We are about to have another baby?"

"Yea."

"Wow."

"That doesn't mean that we are getting back together."

"So, what does it mean."

"It means that we are going to figure it out."

"Oh man. Wait until I tell cuz man." he said excitedly.

"Now, you have two kids on the way, so that will make six kids for you. How are you going to handle it?"

"I'm going to take care of my kids. I got you. Don't worry about that."

I raised my eyebrows, and then I said, "Alright."

He kissed me on the forehead, and then I turned my attention back to Ava.

***

Christmas Eve I showed up to Kyra's party with Ava and Wes. She smiled when she opened the door and saw us together.

"Hello family." she greeted us.

"Hi lady." I said, and then I introduced her to Wes. She told him that it was great to meet him, and then she introduced us to everyone else. Minutes later, Bianca showed up with her boo, and Nikita showed up with Jakari and their son, and then the man of the house appeared from the back of the house.

"To everyone who hasn't met my love. This is my baby Corey."

Everyone spoke to him, and then he made his way around to great people. Corey was extremely handsome, but what shocked me was that he was a white guy. I would have never guessed that her man was not black. He was nicely built, had dark hair, blue eyes, and a huge tattoo on his neck. He seemed nice and friendly and they looked cute together.

More of their friends and family showed up after us. Kyra had a packed house. A mix of Christmas music, soul, and RnB music was playing through her computer speakers. She had cooked a bunch of food, she had treats and toys for the kids, and had given everyone giftbags to take home. Everyone was having a fun time. Even Wes and Jakari. They seemed to be getting along with Kyra's boyfriend. While the guys were talking, Nikita pulled me to the side. We walked out to Kyra's four-seasons porch and sat down on the couch.

Nikita asked, "So, are you two back together?"

"No, but we are figuring things out for this baby."

"Have you told your mom?"

"I'm going to tell her tomorrow. It's going to be a Christmas day surprise."

"Well, I got a surprise for you. I'm pregnant and it's not Jakari's baby."

"Oh my God! What!?" I asked loudly.

"Shhhh. Jakari doesn't know."

"I'm sorry. I'm just shocked Nikita. What the hell?"

"I know, and I don't know what I am going to do. He is married, and I knew the whole time he was married. He never kept that a secret. He knows about Jakari too, but this wasn't supposed to happen."

"Wow Nikita." I said, and then I shook my head.

"Now he wants me to keep it because he claims that he loves me, and he wants to be together."

"How does that make sense? He is married."

"He's talking about leaving our situations and being with each other. I can't uproot my life and move to

Chicago, so I offered to get an abortion, but he doesn't want me to because he says he doesn't believe in them."

"Wow." I said.

"I know. I think that I am just going to tell Jakari that it's his."

"Cousin. Don't do no trifling shit like that." I said.

"Why not? I can't tell Jakari that I was fucking someone else behind his back."

"Why can't you? Be a woman about yours. Don't be like these trifling ass fuck boys."

Nikita shook her head. "I'll let you know what I decide. I might just be getting an abortion and cutting the ball player with the good D off."

"You should just be leaving Jakari's no good ass and be by yourself until you find a good man. Not a married one either."

"Whatever cousin." she said.

The sound of the door caught our attention. Kyra walked out and said, "Hey. I was looking for y'all. We're about to do the Christmas toast."

"Ok. Here we come." I said.

Nikita and I stood up and followed Kyra back into the house.

CHANEL

Chapter 30

The holiday season went by in a flash, and I was angry with Orlando most of it. Orlando and I were doing good after that time I had threatened to divorce him. He took me shopping that day as he promised. He was calling me while he was away. He wasn't turning his phone off. He was being attentive and supportive again. I was doing my wifely duties. I cooked, kept the house clean, had sex with him every day, massaged his body when he was sore, showed up at every home game, and made sure I was home whenever he made it back into town like he asked me to. We even dressed up in couple's costumes for Halloween and hung out with Lisa and Trent. All was good until the week before Thanksgiving.

All his family was set to visit for the holiday. His mom and I were going to cook Thanksgiving dinner together. My mom was going to be in town. I was excited about it. He seemed irritable and uninterested when I was trying to get everything prepared for our visitors. Although his mom, dad, and my mom were staying with us, he had cousins and aunts that were coming in town who weren't going to be staying at our house. I had to help them find flights and hotels and he wasn't helping me with anything. He was constantly on his phone, and then he answered every question I asked with a shrug of his shoulders, or he would say, "I don't know."

A couple of days before the holiday, I was beyond frustrated. Some of his family had already shown up and I was still trying to make sure I had everything we needed for the big dinner. It was the very first family dinner and gathering that we were hosting at our house since our wedding. It was my first-time cooking Thanksgiving dinner ever. I was nervous, and I needed his support, but of course he was too focused on his phone to give me that. I asked him his opinion on a recipe and he shrugged his shoulders while looking at him phone.

I said, "You know this could go a lot smoother if that man of the house would give me his input."

He stood there silent looking at him phone.

"Could you get up out of your phone and pay attention to me once Orlando?" I asked.

He didn't say anything, so I reached and took the phone out of his hand, and then he snapped.

"What the fuck is your problem! Give me my phone Chanel!"

"Oh, now I have your attention?" I asked.

"Give me my phone!" he stepped towards me, so I stepped back.

"I have to take the phone to get my husband to respond to me!?" I asked.

"You are pissing me the fuck off!"

"I asked you for your input on this Thanksgiving get together that you planned that you're not helping with at all!"

"You're acting slow like you can't do shit on your own!"

"I'm slow! I am just asking for a little help from my husband!" I yelled.

"Give me my phone Chanel!"

"Not until you give me some input!"

Right then, he muffed my face with his hand, and knocked me off balance. As I hit the floor, he snatched his phone out of my hand and walked away.

At that moment, I just reacted. I jumped up and ran towards him screaming, "You bastard!"

I started swinging punches at his back. He turned around and back handed me hard so hard that it stopped me in my tracks. I grabbed my face, and then he yelled, "Don't ever take my phone again dumb ass bitch!"

He walked down the hall to his office and shut the door. I started crying uncontrollably. I walked out the garage door, got into my car, and left. I didn't have anywhere to go, so I just drove around the city. I thought about calling the police on him, but I knew if I did that, we would be on TMZ, The Breakfast Club, and possibly Wendy Williams the next morning, and I didn't want that. I thought about getting a hotel room and saying to hell with Thanksgiving dinner. I thought about telling my mom that I canceled dinner, so her and I could hang out, and then I could leave and go back to Minnesota with her. I shook my head back and forth, and then my phone started ringing. I ignored it, and then he called again.

I swiped the screen to answer the call, and then I said, "What Orlando?"

"Where are you?"

"None of your business."

"Come home now."

"I'm not coming back there."

"Come home now Chanel." he said angrily, and then he hung up. I took a deep breath, turned another corner and headed home.

I parked my car in the driveway and walked in the house through the front door. Orlando walked down the stairs and met me by the door with tears in his eyes. He reached out, and I jumped back.

"Baby don't be afraid of me. I'm sorry. I didn't mean to do that." Orlando said. He wrapped his arms around me, squeezed me in a tight hug, and started crying hysterically.

"I don't want to hurt you baby. I don't know why I did that. I have been stressed, and the holidays are hard for me with my grandmother gone. She passed around this time and it always fucks me up you know. That is why I don't have much to say. All this holiday stuff makes me miss her too much. You know that I love you and I want to help baby. Please forgive me. Please."

He looked at me with tears running down his cheeks, and puppy dog eyes. "I love you. I promise that I won't do that again baby. Ok?"

I nodded my head up and down, but I was truly taken aback. That wasn't the person I had just seen thirty minutes prior. He took my hand and walked with me up the stairs to our bedroom. I let him make love to me that night like the situation had never happened.

***

The next morning, I got up early, so that I could pick his mother up from the airport. Orlando had some things planned with his cousin's that day and his mother and I were going grocery shopping for the dinner. When I looked at my reflection in the mirror. I saw a large red circle by my eye where he had back slapped me the night before. I touched it, and then I went to my makeup drawer to find the right concealer to cover it up. As I was doing my make-up, I started telling myself that it was all my fault.

"If I wouldn't have grabbed his phone, this would have never happened. I certainly shouldn't have punched him in the back. I have to learn how to communicate with him in a way that won't make him angry." I said to myself in the mirror, and I believed everything that I was saying.

Chapter 31

After Thanksgiving, I was sure that I figured out how to deal with Orlando. I tried not to fuss and argue with him. I kept up with my wifely duties, and I would hang out with Lisa and the girls while the husbands were out of town. Christmas was around the corner and I was excited to spend time with my husband and exchange gifts, but Orlando was back to the same old stuff. He was barely talking to me when he was at home, but I learned how to work around his bullshit.

The football season was finally ending, and I was excited to have my husband back home with me all the time. I was hoping that we could get some of that spark back that the season took out of our marriage. I was eager to put some spice back into our marriage, so I went out and got this cute little pixie haircut like his favorite singer Rihanna. I was hoping that he would be happy about it and maybe pay attention to me for once. Of course, he didn't acknowledge it until I said something about it. I was disappointed by his reaction, and then he told me a few days later that he loved it, and he just had a lot on his mind. That started to be his normal excuse for most of his behavior.

Christmas Eve had finally arrived, and I was by the tree wrapping gifts for his children. We planned to have them over Christmas Day. We'd bought them so much stuff that gifts were covering half the tree. I still had a bunch of packages to wrap. He wasn't helping as usual, and he was walking around like he had a chip in his shoulder. I knew it was something about not making the playoffs, but I was determined to cheer him up.

"Baby come wrap some gifts with me."

"Nah, I don't feel like it."

"Baby, it will make you feel better."

"I'm good." he said.

I said, "It's just a game baby."

"What?" he asked.

"I said it's just a game. You'll get another chance next season."

Whap!

I fell to the floor and grabbed my face. I didn't even see it coming.

"Don't ever say that it's just a game! This is my life!" he yelled as he was standing over me. "Fuck is wrong with you!"

I started whimpering as I held my face. He grabbed me by my hair and started dragging me away from the tree. "I'ma show you just a game!" he yelled.

"Stop Orlando!" I yelled.

He stopped dragging me and stood over me with his face close to mine and yelled, "Don't ever disrespect me like that again!"

He stepped back, and then I stood up and started running towards the guest bathroom. I slammed the door and locked myself inside. About ten minutes later he started knocking on the bathroom door and talking to me through the door.

"Fuck. I'm sorry baby. I lost it. Please don't cry." he wiggled the handle. "Open the door baby. Please."

I didn't respond. He wiggled the handle again. "Open the door. Please baby. I'm sorry."

"Go away Orlando." I said.

"Aight." I heard him leave. I stayed in the bathroom until. I was sure that he was out of the house. I called Lisa and asked her, if I could come over.

"What's wrong?"

"Nothing I just need to get out of the house for a little while."

"Oh ok. Well, yea I'm not doing anything. Come on."

"Ok." I said. I could tell by the sound of her voice that she knew something was wrong, but she didn't press for more information.

As I was driving to her house Orlando called me begging me to come back home. Lisa lived about an hour away, and I really didn't want to go to go to her house. I didn't want to go home either, and I had nowhere else to go. I had no more money left in my savings. I had depleted my savings account getting necessities for myself, and I was completely depending on Orlando for money, and he knew it. My social networking channel didn't take off like I thought it would, and I basically had nothing, but my car and the stuff I moved into Orlando's house with. I felt stuck and he was on my phone talking me back in.

"I am not coming back there Orlando."

"Baby where are you going?" he asked.

"I am going to Lisa's house."

"Nooo. I don't want you going over there bothering them on Christmas Eve. I don't want Trav and Lisa in our business like that. Come home."

"No Orlando."

"Baby. I'm sorry."

"You've said that before."

"I mean it this time."

"Lisa and Trav's family is over there. They don't need to be in the middle of our shit babe. Come home." Orlando said, and then he sniffled, and then the tears started flowing. "I'm sorry baby. Ok? I told you how it is around the holidays baby. Please don't go over there. I can't have

Trav and Lisa in our business babe. You know I got to see Trav every day."

"Ok. I won't go over there, but I am not coming home."

He sniffled again and said, "Babe you have nowhere to go. You can't be out there in the streets baby. I can't let you leave me. It's Christmas. The kids are coming tomorrow. What am I going to tell them if you're not here?"

"I don't know."

"Just come back baby."

I exhaled, gave into him again, turned the car around, and went back home.

Christmas Day, I gave myself the talk again as I stood in the mirror applying make-up over my new bruise.

"I shouldn't have said anything about the game. I should have just left him alone and let him be in a bad mood. I have to learn to how to pick my battles." I said to my image in the mirror.

An hour later, I was sitting by the Christmas tree watching his kids open their presents with a smile and make-up on my face covering the truth.

Nia Rich

ADARA

Chapter 32

I was sitting on the couch eating a mini bag of Cheetos. Ava was sitting on the couch next to me eating a bag of chips. Christmas was over, and the new year was approaching. The salon was booked solid for the next week, and it was my only day off. I spent the entire day relaxing. Wes called right when I stood up to walk to the kitchen.

When I answered, he said, "Adara."

"What?" I asked.

"I need to stop by right now. It's an emergency."

"What's wrong?"

"Some shit just went down at cuz's house and I need somewhere to be for a few hours. I got to come now Adara please."

I said, "Ok. Come on."

I hung up and took my cup of juice back to the couch. Wes rang my doorbell a few minutes later. I stood up and let him in.

"What's wrong?" I asked.

"Oh man. Cuz was having a little party. Some dumb ass dudes started fighting. We broke the fight up, and then one of them came back and started shooting, and then I bounced and called you. I just need somewhere to chill for a couple of hours until shit dies down."

"I am glad that you're ok Wes. Is your cousin ok?"

"Yes. Everybody is cool, but cuz said the cops is over there right now."

"Ok well. You can stay here. Me and Ava were about to go to bed soon. Do you need to stay the night?"

"I mean, if you don't mind. I'll be out of here in the morning."

"That is fine. I am just glad that you're ok."

Wes exhaled and said, "Me too."

"Anyways. How are you feeling?"

"I'm sleepy, but I am fine."

Wes looked at the bag of chips on the table. "You up in here eating chips?"

I laughed, "Yes. I just had a taste for them."

"You don't even like chips like that, so I know that's my baby that got you eating like that." he said.

I laughed again, and then I said, "Anyways. Do you want to help me put Ava to bed?"

"I got it you just chill." Wes said.

I watched him pick Ava up and walk with in his arms to her room. I thought about what Miles and Kyra said about giving it another chance, and then I went back to watching television.

***

"What the hell is all this stuff in my house?" I asked angrily.

Wes was sitting on the couch waiting for me to get home. I had just walked into my house from work and into a mess. There were boxes and shoes and clothes everywhere. When I left that morning, Wes asked me if he could chill because his cousin said his place was still hot. I knew that meant that cops were still creeping around his house. They were probably driving up and down the block or parked somewhere watching. I told him that he could chill at my place while I was at work, but I didn't say anything about him moving his stuff into my house.

"Adara I can explain." Wes said.

"Please do because I didn't tell you that you could move in."

"Earlier cuz called and told me to come and get some of my stuff because he had a bad feeling, so we packed up most of my stuff and put it in my car. When I got back here, cuz's girl called and said that the feds kicked in the door and took my cousin to jail. I put all my stuff in here because I don't anywhere to put it right now"

I smacked my lips and said, "Wes."

"What? I apologize Adara. I didn't want to bother you at work."

"You couldn't go to your other baby mama's house?"

"Lesley lives with her mom, and I don't fuck with her like that."

I folded my arms, smacked my lips again, and groaned, "Wes.'

Adara, baby, listen. Let me chill here for a minute. I got money, I can help you with shit, and I won't be here for long."

I unfolded my arms, rubbed one of my hands across my forehead, and said, "Oh my God. Wes, I don't know."

"Plus, I can help you out with the Ava now that you are pregnant."

"Wes this is crazy."

"I know Adara. Can you do this for me please? I don't have anywhere else to go."

I took a deep breath, exhaled, and then I said, "Alright."

To be Continued…

Nia Rich

Contact the Author

Email: niarichbooks@gmail.com

F—k Boy 2

Nia Rich

www.ingramcontent.com/pod-product-compliance
Lightning Source LLC
Chambersburg PA
CBHW022003170626
46808CB00001B/267